The Search

Book 1: The Identity Thieves Trilogy

Karen Howard

LEAF BY LEAF

Published by Leaf by Leaf
an imprint of Cinnamon Press,
Lytchett House, 13 Freeland Park, Wareham Road, Poole, Dorset, BH16
6FA
www.cinnamonpress.com

Print Edition ISBN 978-1-78864-871-4
British Library Cataloguing in Publication Data. A CIP record for this
book can be obtained from the British Library.

In the EU, we are fully compliant with GPSR (General Product Safety
Regulation). Our EU GPSR Authorised Representative, via Inpress Books,
is LOGOS EUROPE, 9 rue Nicolas Poussin, 17000, LA ROCHELLE, France
E-mail: Contact@logoseurope.eu

Designed and typeset in Adobe Caslon Pro by Cinnamon Press.
Cover Design Adam Craig.
Cinnamon Press is represented by Inpress.

Karen Howard grew up roaming the Malvern Hills and sampling the delights of Wiltshire. Despite her early love of literature and history, influenced by the books of James Herriot, she chose a scientific path, moving to Plymouth to begin her higher education. Having gained a PhD, she pursued a career in environmental chemistry, publishing a raft of factual papers and ultimately working for a global consultancy.

She travelled widely, spending eight years living partially in France, and began to write creative fiction. Karen takes inspiration from favourite wild and tame landscapes as well as drawing on personal experiences and an unbridled imagination.

In 2014 she self-published her first novel, *The Gimmel Ring*. In 2022, whilst working on the *Identity Thieves Trilogy*, she was awarded an invaluable Cinnamon Pencil creative writing mentorship. *The Search*, the first book of the trilogy, was shortlisted for the Cinnamon Press Literature Award 2023 and New Voices 2025. The second in the series, *The Choice*, was shortlisted for the Cinnamon Press Literature Award 2024. Karen is now working on the concluding novel.

Since retiring in 2021, Karen devotes most of her time to writing, walking and travelling. She lives in Shropshire with her husband and Border Collie.

This book is dedicated to family and friends,
who brighten the world.

The Search

Chapter One

Upton, England, April 1989

In the shadows of the attic Lena kneels before the timeworn steamer trunk, her hands resting on its domed surface. In the meagre light of the single naked bulb dangling unceremoniously from a rafter high up behind her, she reaches for the cloth she brought. She carefully wipes the top and sides of the chest so no dust could speckle its contents on opening. She runs her hands over the pine, stained dark with a hundred passing years. She touches the embossed tin fastenings and leather straps, seeking familiar nicks and burrs. She pauses to smooth a tear from the corner of her eye with the tip of a finger. She knows this will be, must be, the last time if she is ever to mend.

Her fingers come to rest on the brass barrel key. It turns easily in the central lock which has been maintained meticulously. As she unclasps the catches to either side a tremble arises in her core and she waits for it to pass before opening the lid.

Each garment is as immaculate as the day it was worn. Lena lifts each of the items gently, holding them to her face, breathing them, feeling the crisp cotton, soft satin, comforting wool, against her pale skin, allowing herself to remember. Perfect tiny toes between her lips. Fine downy hair, dimpled knees, the determined grip of little fingers. Sunny eyes, adoring and trusting. The scent of milk on translucent skin. Exquisite smiles at once joyful and heart-breaking.

She bows her head, relinquishing her grief.

She doesn't know how much time has passed, only that she feels cold and her face is taut with desiccated tears. She releases a long sigh heavy with regret and inevitability. The moment has come. She removes all the trunk's precious contents, placing them carefully on the clean sheet she brought. She replaces the thin paper lining with sturdier material and restores each item to its rightful place. Lena bites down on her lip as she closes the lid for the final time. Once secure, she pockets the key. Rising stiffly, she moves the container deeper under the eaves and covers it with an off cut of carpet.

She leaves the attic and sits on the edge of her bed. The key to her memories torments her resolve as she rotates it between thumb and fingers. She knows what she should do, what she promised when she made the bargain with herself. Then she exits her flat, stepping down a narrow flight of stairs leading to a door that gives onto the high street. It's a quiet afternoon and Jake is likely to be in the stockroom. Even so she takes care to avoid walking past their shop front. Nothing must detract from her purpose. No questions can be asked.

Within minutes she comes to the quay where the persistent morning mist clings in patches to the surface of the river. No one is there, save an elderly man walking a Dalmatian further along the bank. Lena shivers; she has come without her coat, a single purpose on her mind. She takes the key out of her pocket; in that moment it comes to signify everything that has passed in recent years. She raises it above her head in readiness to consign to the depths of the water. Yet she cannot bring herself to do it. To abandon their memories is to desert them. She can try to protect herself from further damage but can't turn her back on them, ever. She makes up her mind to give the key to Jake to hide somewhere, safe from discovery by her.

Lena thinks then of her beloved little Sarah and smiles. Fate has been benevolent and callous in turns but has also conceded a reprieve. It will soon be time to collect her daughter from nursery. She closes her eyes for a moment and Sarah comes into view—running to meet her, arms outstretched, one hand clutching a colourful painting on ragged paper—and her heart fills with happiness once more.

I'll always do everything in my power to safeguard you, my beautiful girl. No one'll ever love you more than me.

Chapter Two

Malvern, England, 5 May 2018

Saturday had started out as a perfectly ordinary day. Why wouldn't it? Sarah had stood on tiptoes to kiss her boyfriend, Ben, cheerio, answered a text from her best friend, Jennifer, arranging their next get-together and checked her emails in case there was anything urgent for her projects at the laboratory that needed immediate attention.

The day was warm and bright and the large, wooded form of Summer Hill behind the cottages sheltered them from the gathering south-west breeze. Oak, birch and ash whispered to each other through intermingled branches spread protectively over swathes of bluebells and wild garlic. On mornings such as these, Sarah was in the habit of sitting with a coffee outside her front door to absorb the stunning view east over Malvern Common and beyond to the wide fertile plain through which the river Severn purposefully cut its passage. On the common large areas of golden brown were giving way to green as new bracken fronds unfurled through last year's growth and the rich grassland between the bracken hosted patches of yellow bird's-foot-trefoil.

Sarah looked at her watch; it was past eleven and there

were things to do. She briefly checked herself in the hall mirror, ran her fingers through her short blonde hair, accentuating the spikes and dark low-lights and coloured her full lips a sienna red, before driving the seven miles to her parents' house in the small town of Upton-on-Severn. She'd promised to collect the post from the porch and water the plants while Jake and Lena Lester were away exploring the Pacific islands and New Zealand for eight weeks. Their camping and outdoor gear business had prospered over the years, allowing them to move from a small flat above the shop in the high street to a smart house overlooking the river. The road was quiet as it eventually narrowed to a footpath that ran alongside the water for miles. Sarah loved the house where she'd happily spent many of her formative years. She'd been delighted to move back to the area from Oxfordshire, where she'd lived with her former partner, Rob. That relationship hadn't ended well; her best memories of Oxford were of securing a position with an oil-spill consultancy, followed by promotion, and meeting Ben at the gym. They'd fallen deeply for each other. Thankfully Ben was flexible about location so, when the chance came along to move to the company's site in Malvern, she'd jumped at it.

Sarah pushed envelopes aside with the front door as she entered her parents' house, shut the door and bent to pick up the post. In the kitchen were two boxes on the floor, a scrawled note left on top of one saying *Charity shop—if you get a chance.* Her parents were thinking they might downsize and had been having a sort-out. They'd asked Sarah if she would look through some of the containers in the loft and take anything she wanted to keep. Sarah couldn't bear to think of them moving from this house yet she wasn't too worried. Organising and decluttering were things they did from time to time. They'd threatened to move before but never had.

She gathered a watering can from the conservatory and fulfilled her duty. Then she climbed into the loft to look for her boxes of childhood things. Her parents wanted to keep her school reports and the cards and letters she'd written to them. They also had precious photographs in a metal filing cabinet, which were to stay. Sarah had been tasked with removing her old doll's house, toys and various teenage belongings, including her sizeable collection of detective stories and three albums of pressed flowers. She located the former, moved it nearer to the loft entrance and began searching for her other possessions. Her mother was a methodical, tidy person who hated mess, hence many of the cardboard boxes were clearly labelled, making Sarah's job easier. She located the photos she'd taken with her first camera and her teenage diaries easily, resisting the temptation to look through everything there and then; the loft was cold and she was looking forward to spending time at home sifting through the memories and sharing them with Ben. There didn't seem to be a box labelled 'Toys', but she recalled an old trunk of playthings that her parents used to keep in the living room. She hunted for it in the dusty corners under the rafters, throwing shadows across exposed lagging in the dim light of the single bulb. At length she located a small brown wooden trunk hidden under a piece of carpet. She lifted it by its leather handles into the centre of the space, underneath the light.

Sarah sat cross-legged in front of the old domed chest. A third of the distance from either end was a metal clasp, fixed via a small central lock. She tried opening the clasps but they were fastened tightly. She searched the area, but there was no key. She didn't remember it ever being locked when she had put her teddies to bed in it. She sighed. She'd have to get it home and try to open it there. She manoeuvred the box through the loft hatch from underneath and managed to slide it down the ladder. Eventually she succeeded in collecting all her belongings and loaded them into her car. Locking up, Sarah was satisfied she'd aided her parents' clear-out.

Ben arrived home late afternoon and helped Sarah carry her belongings into the lounge. She stacked her rediscovered whodunnits on the bottom shelf of a tall oak bookcase in the only available space, next to her hardbacks on cookery, her well-thumbed plant and butterfly identification handbooks and a series of walking guides. She tutted; she must reorder her collection more logically. All the while an appetising aroma escaped from the kitchen. Ben would often create tasty dinners in the slow cooker before he left for work to be ready for them that evening. Sarah usually cooked at weekends, today being an exception, experimenting with recipes and stocking the freezer with appetising meals for future consumption. Today Ben was making a delicious chicken casserole they then enjoyed unhurriedly with a bottle of Carménère.

Afterwards they sat on the floor with the boxes, backs against the sofa, and looked at the photographs Sarah had brought. Sarah's first camera, given to her on her tenth birthday, had produced imprecise small square images which had not retained their colour well. In the box containing her photos she also discovered a bag of old prints belonging to her parents, with a cardboard folder containing her school reports. Sarah noted that her mother's usually thorough organisation must have slipped and was glad of it. She and Ben went into fits of laughter on seeing pictures of Sarah as a child in various compromising positions: with one foot stuck down a rabbit hole; covered in snow having fallen face down in a drift; caught unawares picking her nose; on the beach having been soaked by an unexpectedly large wave. Among the funny photos there were also pictures of her parents and of the three of them together celebrating memorable occasions; birthdays, at Christmas and enjoying the Malvern Hills through the seasons and across the years. Sarah reminisced to Ben about the various events depicted in the snapshots.

After a while, however, Ben fell silent and withdrawn. Sarah was lost in her own recollections, so didn't notice straight away. It was when he returned into the room after pouring them both a glass of port that she recognised the mix of sorrow and forced cheerfulness on his face each time she showed him another print. His mouth was pulled into a smile, but his eyes told a different story. He was obviously fighting to stay positive and deflect the memories of his own childhood. She chided herself inwardly for being so thoughtless; all this family happiness laid out before him was reminding him of his very different upbringing. She knew he didn't begrudge her contentment for a moment but realised he'd be wishing he could shut out his past completely and keep it locked away, as he'd confided to her once. As he sat beside her again, she hugged him.

'God, I'm so sorry, Ben. I've been going on and on about my family, being so self-centred. I didn't think.'

'It's okay,' he replied selflessly, 'you shouldn't have to apologise for a happy childhood.'

'No, but it's not fair of me to prattle on about what a great time I had when you were in and out of children's homes and having such a rough life. So, I'm sorry,' Sarah said determinedly. 'Come on, let's drink our port and I'll put the photos away.'

Ben nodded. 'Then we'll see if we can open that trunk, shall we?'

It took Ben some time, deftly using a piece of wire, to persuade the little lock to yield. As it did so Ben grinned sheepishly. 'A facet of my misspent youth.'

Sarah raised her eyebrows at him. He sat back and let her undo the metal clasps. They sprang open with a click and the trunk was ready to divulge its secrets. Sarah slowly raised the lid and discovered it was not full of her toys as expected. At first glance the box seemed to be full of clothes. 'Oh,' she said, confused and slightly disappointed.

'Perhaps the toys are underneath,' suggested Ben.

'It used to be so full of dolls and teddies and board games that I had to squash them in. Perhaps Mum and Dad got rid of some.'

Sarah took out the first item and held it up: a little yellow sundress with a big red flower sown onto the bottom right. 'I remember this dress. It was my favourite when I was about three or four. I used to think I could press the flower and make a wish,' she said. 'I didn't know Mum and Dad had kept it. How lovely.'

'Cute,' nodded Ben.

The next layer consisted of some knitted booties, a white cotton bonnet and two baby-grows, one pink and one blue. 'Hedging their bets,' joked Ben, tilting his head at the tiny onesies as Sarah lifted them out of the trunk and placed them carefully on the sofa. She didn't reply; she was staring at the next item of clothing. It was an exquisite pale blue satin jacket and trouser set edged with lace: a christening suit.

Sarah put her hands to her mouth. 'Oh, God,' she exclaimed through her fingers.

'What is it? What's the matter?'

She took her fingers away from her face and clasped her hands. 'My parents once told me that they'd had a little boy.' She looked up at Ben sadly. 'He died before I was born. He was only two or three, I think. These must be his christening clothes.' She ran her fingers lightly over the beautiful material. 'Christ, it must have been terrible for them. How do you ever get over something like that?'

'They love you so fiercely. Perhaps that's a part of it,' Ben observed.

Sarah sighed. 'Poor Mum and Dad.'

'They're lucky to have you,' Ben remarked gently, 'as you are to have them.'

Sarah raised her head and breathed in audibly. 'Yes,' she agreed purposefully, laying a hand on his arm. 'We're all lucky to have one another.' She lifted the little suit and, as she did, one of the pearl-effect buttons fell off the jacket and rolled into the bottom of the trunk. She felt around for it unsuccessfully. 'Blast. Never mind, I'll find it later when this is empty.'

Next was a petite christening gown of embroidered lace overlaying an ivory satin underskirt, with pretty little puff sleeves. Sarah gasped as she held it aloft. 'Wow, that's gorgeous. I guess it must have been mine.' As she turned the dress the delicate flowers embellishing the lace caught the light, seeming to shimmer. She placed the gown carefully with the blue suit.

The following item was a white blanket with a teddy bear embroidered on it, which was covering several lumpy shapes in the bottom of the trunk. On removing the blanket, she found a diminutive round wooden pot with a tight-fitting lid containing a lock of copper-brown hair and a seven-coin proof set from 1985 in mint condition. There was also a tiny porcelain vessel with a hinged top, decorated with an image of Mrs Tiggy-Winkle, in which lay a lock of blonde hair. Sarah assumed the coppery hair must have belonged to her brother as her hair had always been blonde. Having removed the remaining contents she sat back on her heels, observing the items now surrounding her.

'That's a delightful collection of precious things,' she remarked. 'God knows where the toys are, though. I think I'll save the school reports until tomorrow.' She grinned at Ben. 'Then we can both have another laugh.'

'Good idea,' he agreed. 'I bet they're nothing like mine though. I never delivered them although I expect the schools got wise to that in the end and sent them straight to my foster carers. The only thing I enjoyed and was any good at was sport.'

'Yeah... and you did do well at that, didn't you?' Sarah replied supportively, thinking how hard he'd worked to build a private fitness instruction business as well as working as a gym instructor and swim coach at a local health club.

'Not bad. A man has to be good at something,' Ben laughed, then paused. 'It was my haven,' he added reflectively. 'Look, why don't you put those things back while 1 make us a cup of rum hot chocolate. Oh and don't forget the button that fell off. I guess it needs to be sewn back on before we put the trunk away in your parents' loft.'

'Sounds like a plan,' agreed Sarah, smiling, 'I could do with a choc and a tot.' She looked in the bottom of the trunk, but the button wasn't there. She shook out each item of clothing then refolded them, searched the sofa and scoured the lounge carpet in case the button had dropped out when she'd removed any of the other objects but it was nowhere to be seen. She felt around the inside of the trunk, which was lined with old magnolia wallpaper, making it hard to pick out a tiny object of roughly the same colour, but it wasn't there. As she ran her fingers around the bottom perimeter one more time the index finger on her right hand connected with a little hole in the bottom right-hand corner of the base of the trunk. She felt something cold and metallic and pressed down on it. As she did so she heard a click and the base section sprung up a few millimetres. The trunk had a false bottom! The other side was still fixed, the wallpaper covering any such mechanism. Sarah felt around until she found a small indentation and pressed into it hopefully. Sure enough, there was a click and the base was freed, pulling slightly at the paper covering.

As Ben returned with mugs of steaming chocolate, Sarah was gingerly lifting the false base. 'Look what I found,' she exclaimed excitedly.

'Bloody hell, a secret compartment? You only read about those in books. Aren't your parents the dark horses?' Ben responded animatedly. He turned around to deposit their drinks on the sideboard.

Sarah's enjoyment clouded. 'I don't understand,' she frowned, holding up another christening gown identical to the first. With it were another set of white knitted booties, a yellow cotton bonnet and another pink baby-grow. A tiny square porcelain box decorated with a picture of Jemima Puddleduck and containing a lock of blonde hair completed the set. 'There are two identical christening gowns. If my brother wore the blue suit when he was christened, why are there two dresses? And there's another lock of hair, look.' She stared at the items a few more moments, a dreadful theory forming in her mind. Sarah looked up at Ben, dismayed. 'Oh God… there must have been another child, a girl.'

Ben came to sit beside her, placing an arm around her shoulders.

'No one would have identical gowns unless they were intended to be used at the same time. You'd only need two identical dresses if you have twins.'

Sarah instinctively knew something was wrong about this collection of belongings. Clearly there'd been another baby, a twin, she didn't know about, that her parents hadn't told her about. It was unlike her parents to keep secrets from her. They all had an extremely close relationship and her upbringing had been happy and honest. That they wouldn't share with her something as important as this was incomprehensible. And something else disturbed her, but she couldn't bear to voice her thoughts. Why were these things deliberately hidden while the others were in the main compartment of the trunk? This spoke to her of a conscious decision to keep her in ignorance. She felt deceived then upset that she should think so.

Ben shifted his position on the carpet, pointing to a

small white envelope which lay half-hidden under the woollen booties. 'Look there's something else.'

Sarah hesitated. 'I'm not sure we should be looking at all this. I mean, these things aren't ours and they've obviously been hidden for a reason.' She ran her hands through her hair while she contemplated the situation. Ben gestured his acquiescence. It was her call; he wouldn't interfere.

After a few moments Sarah shook her head, contradicting herself. 'But now we've found them I have to understand…' her voice trailed off. Her hands were shaking as she extracted the thin paper packet. It was sealed. 'I can't… tear it… but… I need to know,' she said apprehensively.

'I could steam it open, if you like?' Ben spoke softly, at once giving her the opportunity to discover the contents and reseal the envelope and to remove herself from the actual act.

Sarah nodded, tight-lipped, and passed the envelope to him.

He pressed his lips to hers, then rose and left the room. As she heard the kettle coming to the boil Sarah ran her hands over her face and breathed in deeply.

Eventually Ben returned to sit on the floor beside her. 'Come and sit here,' he indicated the space between his legs. 'Whatever is in here we'll tackle it together, okay?'

She snuggled up to him gratefully and he held her loosely around the waist as she drew a document out of the envelope and unfolded it. It was a birth certificate.

The baby's name on the document was 'Suzette Rose Gregory' with the surname corrected to 'Lester' and in the date of birth column was written 'Twentieth of

September, Nineteen eighty-five'. Jake and Lena were given as the parents and the place of birth as Ullapool.

'That's my birthday. I was born in Ullapool,' Sarah cried before clapping a hand over her mouth. A surge of adrenalin rushed through her body and she felt lightheaded. She scrambled to her feet, thrusting the certificate at Ben and ran out of the room, 'Oh my God… oh my God!'

'Where are you going?' Ben jumped up and dashed after her.

Taking the steps two at a time, Sarah sprinted upstairs to retrieve her birth certificate from a box file she kept on a shelf in the spare bedroom which doubled as a little office. She was opening the document when Ben reached her.

'Look. They're almost identical,' she panted excitedly as they held the certificates side by side. 'Same date, same place of birth, same parents' names, same surname correction in the margin when my parents got married, same marriage details and occupations, same everything. Jesus, look at the times of birth.'

Ben followed her finger as Sarah pointed to the entries written under the date of birth. One read 8:10 a.m. and the other 8:25 a.m. 'But… this means you're…'

'Yes,' interrupted Sarah, momentarily exhilarated. 'I'm a twin! My God. I can't believe it. A twin.'

Then she sank to the floor, dazed and unable to take in any more information. 'But… why didn't they tell me?' she eventually uttered quietly; her head bowed. 'What happened to her… to Suzette Rose?' Despite the warmth of the cottage, Sarah shivered. The skin on her arms was cool and clammy and she felt the heat drain from her face.

'Did she die? Was she adopted by someone else for some reason?' She turned her face to Ben, her hazel eyes glistening. 'I don't remember her.'

Ben helped her to her feet. 'Come on,' he said practically, 'let's get you downstairs and warm you up with a hot drink.' He settled her on the sofa under a quilt and made her another hot chocolate, this time without the alcohol. He carefully placed the contents of the trunk back roughly as they had originally been positioned, keeping out the birth certificate.

Sarah sipped her drink for a while, staring into space, lost in a murky whirlwind of thoughts, none particularly defined. At length she pronounced, 'I have to speak to Mum and Dad.'

Ben sat and put his arm around her shoulder, giving her a squeeze. 'Yes. Only they have the explanation. But I think you should wait a while, get your thoughts together. You've had a big shock. You need to think what to say to them. It's not going to be easy on the phone.'

Sarah nodded and slowly finished the remainder of her hot chocolate. Then she said, trying for calm, 'I have to talk to them tonight.' She looked at her watch. 'I'm not sure where they'll be, Tahiti maybe.' She put a hand to her forehead. 'Or maybe they haven't got that far yet; all I know is that they're island hopping. So let's say they're in Tahiti, they'll be… what… ten or eleven hours behind? That's ten or eleven thirty in the morning.'

'Are you alright?' asked Ben, concernedly.

'I think so,' she gave him a half-smile and shook her head slightly. 'I really don't know what to think or how to feel right now. I need to hear Mum and Dad.'

'Okay, stay there. I'll get you the phone,' answered Ben.

Chapter Three

Sarah had been trying to contact her parents for two days, without success and had left messages hoping they were having a lovely holiday and asking them to ring her as soon as they could. At around seven in the evening on Monday she received the desired call.

'Sarah! Hello, darlin',' Lena spoke excitedly.

'You sound a bit faint. Can you get nearer the phone?'

'Hello, love.' It was her dad this time. Jake still had a slight West-country drawl matching his wife's, a dialect diluted over the years he'd been absent from Devon. 'How's my favourite girl? Oh wait a minute I'd better compliment yer mother or she'll get jealous.' His voice became distant, as if he'd turned away, but Sarah made out the words: 'You're my favourite too, old girl.'

'Hey, less of the old you cheeky beggar,' shouted her mum in the background.

Jake's voice became clear again. 'All these women vyin' for my attention, I dunno.'

'There're only two, Dad.'

I know, but a man's gotta dream,' he laughed. So how's things with you? Found the silver yet? Don't sell it, yer mum needs it for the next big trip. Second thoughts, she might need it for this one—she's goin' through the vanilla punch like nobody's business; didn't know there was that much rum on the island.'

A tut ensued, followed by a muffled, 'Give me that.' Then her mum's voice. 'Hello, my luvver. Anyone'd think yer dad's been on the rum and it's barely eight o'clock here.'

Sarah managed to get a few words in. 'Where are you exactly?

'We reached Maupiti yesterday evening. We'll spend a few days here then move on to Bora Bora. We flew here from Tahiti, but we're gonna do most of the shorter crossings by ferry. We're workin' our way east. It's so beautiful, Sarah. This island's just four square miles, an' so peaceful, but we can snorkel an' dive an' we're plannin' to walk up the volcano if I feel fit enough. It's like paradise. Dunt seem real.'

'Yes, I have t' keep pinching yer mother so she knows she's not dreaming,' Jake interjected, sounding someway off again.

'Can you put the phone on speaker so we can all hear each other at the same time?' Sarah suggested, exasperation building, though she kept it from her tone.

'We can try, but I dunt think the signal's particularly good here. Did I say we're in a wooden hut on stilts with a thatched roof? Tis gorgeous but a bit basic. Hang on, is that better? Yer dad did promise me a bit o' luxury and I'm still waitin' for it.' There followed a muffled 'Ooph,' as if Lena had elbowed Jake in the ribs.

'I bought you a bigger tent, what're you complainin' about? In any case there's no campsite here so you've got the posh accommodation,' Jake chuckled.

'Sounds like you're having a fabulous time.' Her parents were so excited and happy that Sarah tried to make small talk for a few minutes more, asking questions about the islands and their plans, all the while trying to work out how to begin what she had to say, her consideration waning and her courage diminishing. She'd imagined their conversation time and again in her head over the past couple of days, but hearing their joyful voices was off-putting. Then her chance came to change the tack of the conversation.

'Oh, before I forget, did you find yer trunk of toys?' asked her father. 'I put it in the garage for you. I thought it was a bit heavy for you to bring down from the loft. I can't remember whether I told you.'

The penny dropped. They must have two wooden trunks and she'd misremembered which was hers. Sarah took a deep breath before replying. 'No, you didn't tell me and I didn't look in the garage. Actually, I found what I thought was my toy trunk in the loft and brought it back home… and I opened it.'

Sarah waited nervously for a response.

There was a long pause and Sarah could hear some murmuring, she thought it was her mum whispering, 'but it's locked.' She decided to continue. 'I'm sorry, but I've seen what's in it. I thought it had my toys inside. It's lovely that you've kept those precious things.'

'Sarah, love, I don't know how you managed to open it without a key, but it dunt matter. Of course we've kept some baby things; they're of huge sentimental value to us,' her dad replied gently.

'I'm sorry. I know I shouldn't have looked through the contents. But I discovered some by accident, I really did.' Sarah paused, then burst out, 'I need to know who Suzette Rose is.'

There was an anguished cry on the end of the phone and her dad uttered 'Lena, darlin'. After another long pause he addressed Sarah, his voice serious and closer, the mobile obviously no longer in speaker mode. 'Love, your mum's upset, it's difficult for her. We can't talk about this now.'

But Sarah persisted. She had to know. 'It was a shock for me, Dad. I've seen the birth certificate. I need to know. Am I a twin?'

Silence again.

'Dad, please!'

'Oh, Christ. Yes… you are. Suzette Rose was your sister.' Jake spoke quietly, trying for calm, but there was a distinct tremor in his voice. Sarah could sense he was shaken. 'I'm sorry you had to find out. We kept it from you to protect you.'

Sarah became more anxious. 'What do you mean, protect me? Did she die? What happened to her?'

'Yes love, she did die… when she was very young,' her father responded softly. He searched for the right words. 'We… it… well, it was a horrendous time… and you were merely a baby. You didn't know any different an' there was no point upsettin' you when you were older or draggin' it all up again for us,' he justified. 'So… there it is. You know now.'

Sarah felt as if she'd been kicked in the stomach. To have just discovered that she'd had a twin only for her worst theory to be confirmed seemed a cruel twist of fate. She had found and lost her twin in the space of two days. She pulled her knees up to her chest, resting her head in her free hand, and remained silent, cocoon-like, for a few moments. She felt cheated and greatly saddened. She could never know her sister. The sensation was different from knowing she'd once had a brother who'd died before she was born. Suzette Rose was her twin, a part of her. They'd shared the same womb, the same genes. They would have been alike. There was still so much she didn't know—she had so many questions but didn't know where to begin.

After a while she vaguely heard her mother's voice asking if she was alright, although for a few moments the sound seemed muffled as if reaching her through cotton wool. Her mum's words became more insistent. 'Sarah, darlin', answer me, please.'

As she registered the question Sarah felt a rush of frustration sweep through her body. She was impatient to know more, but sensitivity chose the initial words she spoke. Her voice emerged as a whisper. 'I can't imagine how it must feel to lose a baby. I understand why you didn't tell me when I was a child, but now I'm an adult you can share it with me; you don't need to protect me anymore. What I don't understand is why you didn't tell me about Suzette when you told me about George.' Her timbre began to rise. 'Surely it's even more important for me to know that I once had a twin sister. I know it must be upsetting for you to think about it, but I need to know how she died. How old was she?'

Her mother began to cry softly. 'Darlin', we love you—that's all you need to think about. She… you were both… very young, only…' she broke off, unable to continue.

'You were only nineteen months,' Jake finished his wife's response. 'Look, love, we'll tell you everythin' you need to know when we get back. I'm sorry we're so far away right now. This is difficult for all of us over the phone. We'll talk about it when we return, okay?'

Sarah persisted, anger beginning to penetrate her tone. 'Dad, I know you don't want to talk about it, and I'm sorry to ask, but questions have been going round and round in my head for the last couple of days. Could you please tell me how my sister died?'

There was a long pause before Jake was able to answer. Sarah heard him breathing heavily but didn't want to say anything more. She waited impatiently, allowing him time to collect himself.

'Love, it happened suddenly. She went to sleep and didn't wake up. It's called "sudden and unexpected death in childhood",' Jake said sadly.

'Do you mean like… cot death?' Sarah faltered.

'Yes, like that, but they dunt call it that when the child's a bit older.'

'Dad, I'm so sorry.'

Jake sighed unhappily. 'It was a long time ago. You were so young. We didn't know how to tell you. I think we said your sister had gone t' sleep. We didn't talk about it with you after that because we didn't want you to remember and be upset.'

'I'm sure you managed it the best way you could,' Sarah responded, experiencing an upwelling of compassion. 'It must have been unbearable for you, especially having lost your firstborn as well. I can't imagine…' she broke off, momentarily lost for words.

'Sarah, love, you know we'd never knowin'ly hurt you; you're more precious to us than life,' he stated devotedly. 'I'm sorry you had to find out this way. Perhaps we should have told you once you were eighteen. But… we couldn't bear… to drag it all up again. Your mum's never quite got over it.'

'I'm sorry, Dad. I don't want to hurt you by talking about it. I won't mention it to Mum again. I just… needed to know.'

'I understand, love. It's important to you. She was yer sister after all. But it's better if we leave her in peace and live our lives to the full, the best way we can,' Jake responded gently.

'Yes,' Sarah agreed, 'but I have one more question, if you don't mind?'

'Of course, love.'

'Did she, Suzette, die at home, or somewhere else?' she asked hesitantly.

'She was at home, in Scotland; a place where she was always happy,' her father replied tearfully. After a hesitation he continued, his tone becoming brighter, clearly trying to recover himself. 'Look, we've gotta go now. We'll talk again soon. You take care. Give our love to Ben.'

'Bye, darlin'… we love you,' came her mum's broken voice.

'Love you both too. Bye.'

Sarah put down the phone and sobbed.

Nine thousand miles away in French Polynesia Jake and Lena sat side by side on a palm studded beach staring at a turquoise lagoon but not seeing, each lost in the events of the past, trapped in their own minds but sharing the distress of their daughter's discovery. They'd hoped this day would never come.

Lena cuddled into Jake's shoulder, trying to calm herself, her pain fresh as the day she was first stricken with it, a deep wound barely healed. He rocked her gently in his arms like a child. She felt her anxiety draw itself over her forehead and pull at the corners of her eyes and mouth. Her heart was thumping. At length, she raised her head and fixed her eyes on him.

'What else could I have said?' Jake looked as though he'd aged twenty years in as many minutes. He rubbed his chin through his grey beard, trying to think.

Lena sighed wretchedly. 'How am I gonna face her when we get home? Oh, God, I hoped we'd never have to do this.'

Jake tried to comfort his wife. 'Look, love, she already knew about one child who died, a siblin' she never knew. This is the same. She dunt remember Suzette. She was far too young to recollect anythin' about her. Suzette was our loss, not Sarah's, an' we agreed long ago how to cope with that loss. An' now we decide what Sarah can know an' what we keep from her,' he said calmly and firmly. 'She'll feel a little sad knowin' that she had a twin sister who died, but she won't grieve for a person she never knew.'

'We've had to lie to her. If she keeps asking questions I'm not sure I can do it again,' Lena sobbed.

'We have no choice, love,' Jake's voice was strained. 'You know that as well as I do. We made our bed long ago,' he continued sadly, 'now we do what's best for Sarah.'

Chapter Four

Sarah lay awake in the small hours, questions nagging, pulling at her thoughts, twisting them this way and that and moving them around in circles until she couldn't separate them. Her father's explanation still didn't make sense. They hadn't wanted to upset her or themselves, yet they'd felt able tell her about George's death some years ago. Why him but not Suzette? Surely they'd have been as upset about one child as the other? Why didn't they mention Suzette at the same time? They hadn't explained why Suzette's possessions were hidden away from the others, deliberately separated and concealed. There was plenty of room in the main compartment of the trunk for everything. She listened to her intuition—her parents weren't telling her the whole truth. This was unsettling. It felt like a betrayal of the tacit honesty between them. For the second time Sarah experienced a sense of separation from her parents; a fissure in their hitherto steadfast relationship. It was a new undermining sensation and she didn't like it.

The aromas of coffee brewing, bacon sizzling and buttered toast reached Sarah in the bedroom as she threw on a T-shirt and combed her hair. She had flexitime owing to her at work and had left the laboratory administrator a voicemail the previous evening saying she'd not be in until the afternoon. Ben realised she'd had another restless night and left her to sleep whilst he prepared a late breakfast. The delicious smells from the kitchen were beginning to make her stomach rumble and she craved a cup of coffee. However, before going downstairs she retrieved her birth certificate from its box file and made a copy, along with Suzette's certificate, which she'd filed temporarily with hers. She replaced the originals and took the copies down to the kitchen. As she'd showered, she'd decided what to do. She would need to visit her parents' house again.

The sun was shining through the kitchen windowpanes, illuminating the tasty bacon and eggs with a warm golden glow. Ben's shift at the gym didn't begin until two that afternoon and he'd opted to accompany Sarah to Upton. They needed to search Jake and Lena's personal documents. Ben had checked the envelope containing Suzette's birth certificate and also thoroughly examined the trunk, but there was no other documentation hidden there.

They drove to Upton beside fields of vibrant fresh pasture and young spring barley, through elongated villages, between thick tall hedgerows and past several farmsteads. After fifteen minutes or so the road and the river converged to run alongside each other and Upton's distinctive old stone clock tower came into view. Sarah turned her Toyota Prius into Church Street and headed for the quay, past the pretty jumble of old Tudor and Georgian buildings. As it was such a bright sunny day the eateries on Waterside were busy and people spilled out to enjoy their refreshments overlooking the river. Sarah took a short cut through a narrow lane which eventually led to the river and her parents' home. She pulled into the small parking space opposite a large willow tree on the riverbank.

Once inside the house, Sarah and Ben began with the dark green metal filing cabinet in the attic. Thanks to her mother's meticulous nature all of its hanging folders were labelled in small, neat handwriting and ordered alphabetically. Sarah located a folder helpfully marked 'Certificates' and removed it. Ben began looking through the papers it contained, using the torch app on his phone to supplement the meagre glow from the loft light. Sarah continued searching the cabinet for anything else that might pertain to Suzette. She found a folder marked 'Ullapool' but it was empty apart from a scrap of paper containing a telephone number. Sarah removed the folder from the cabinet.

'Have you found anything?' she asked Ben impatiently.

Ben looked up and shook his head, his blonde curls accentuated by the motion and the momentary flash of torchlight which shone through them as he moved. 'No, nothing with the name Suzette on it. There are five death certificates here; one for George Lester who died when he was two.'

'My brother.' Sarah shook her head sadly. 'Two, my God.'

'There are also records for a Carol Lester in 1991 and a Thomas Lester in 1998,' Ben continued.

'My grandparents,' Sarah affirmed.

'A death certificate for a David Gregory dated 1978.'

'Mum's dad. He died when Mum was in her teens,' Sarah replied.

'And a Judith Gregory, dated 2006.'

'Grandma, Mum's mum, bless her. That's it? Anything else?'

'Nothing more, sweetheart,' Ben returned gravely. 'There are other certificates—your parents' marriage, a copy of your birth record, your brother's birth—but nothing with the name Suzette on it.' He frowned momentarily. 'It's odd that George's surname is recorded as Lester on his certificates while yours says Gregory amended to Lester.'

'Hmm. I remember questioning why I had an alteration on my birth certificate. Mum said it was because I was registered with her surname and it was changed after they got married some years later. Apparently, the original details on a Scottish birth certificate can't be changed. The correction is documented separately and then you can get a new birth certificate with the amendment added. But that doesn't explain why my brother's surname was recorded as Lester.' She shrugged. 'Maybe Dad registered him and assumed he'd be a Lester.'

'Perhaps, when you were registered, she was pissed off with him for not marrying her.'

Sarah managed a smile.

Ben pressed his lips together and looked at Sarah sympathetically. 'It does seem strange the birth certificate for your twin wasn't filed with all these others.'

'Yes,' Sarah agreed despondently, 'and if she's dead where's her death certificate and why wasn't it in the trunk hidden with her birth certificate? I can't understand it. Mum and Dad have always been so straight with me.' She shrugged and turned her hands palm upwards frustratedly. 'I mean, why go to such lengths to hide her documentation? It doesn't make sense.'

'Maybe they mistakenly filed her death certificate somewhere else?' Ben suggested weakly. 'Let's look in the folders either side of the "Certificates" file.' Sarah pulled out more hanging files, handing some to Ben and he took them to the space under the light to look through, sitting cross-legged on the dusty floorboards. Privately he doubted that a document as important as this would have been misfiled. If it was going to be anywhere, he reckoned it would have been hidden with the birth certificate which had been most purposefully concealed, though goodness knows why. It wasn't at all characteristic of Sarah to go rummaging around in her parents' belongings, so private papers would have remained private, in all likelihood, and there should be no need to go to great lengths to secrete documents in hidden compartments. He'd only known Jake and Lena two years, but they had fervently welcomed him into their family and now treated him like a son. They were the only people, apart from Sarah, he had allowed himself to trust completely. Sarah was right; there was something perplexing about this, although for her sake he didn't want to concede that without investigating all the options. Sarah had an intimate relationship with her folks and he hoped with all his heart that there was a simple explanation.

Ultimately, they searched through the entire cabinet for the missing death certificate but it was nowhere to be found. Sarah suggested that perhaps it had been lost when the family moved from Ullapool. It was possible, of course.

They drove back to Malvern mostly in silence, each lost

in their own thoughts. Sarah was to drop him off at the gym as there wasn't time for them to go home to retrieve his car before his shift. On reaching the outskirts of the town Sarah stated resolutely, 'Plan B then,' her attempt at optimism unfortunately belied by her countenance.

'Yep, plan B,' Ben concurred, smiling at her supportively and squeezing her leg.

They arrived at the gym car park. He reached over and pulled her towards him, giving her a bear hug then stroking her cheek with the back of his fingers. 'It'll be okay, you know. We'll get to the bottom of it. There's nothing we can't overcome together.'

Left alone with his heartening words, Sarah was reminded of the reassuring nature of their relationship and thanked fate for bringing them together. On the way to work she rang Jennifer in North Yorkshire using the hands-free phone and told her about the discovery of her twin. Her closest pal had known Jake and Lena since she was five, when they'd been schoolmates.

'Bloody hell, Sarah. I'm so sorry. I agree with you, it's uncharacteristic of your parents to keep such a secret. How much they love you has always been obvious. You're so close.

'I know. I can't understand it. I don't know what to do, Jen.'

'I was concerned the moment I heard your voice, the lack of your usual spark. But, Sarah, you're strong,' Jennifer emphasised. 'You've continually been the more resilient of us, taking life's knocks on the chin and fighting back twice as hard. You know it's barely three years since you supported me through that nightmare. Ever since, I've determined to make the most of every day and I'm succeeding, thanks in no small part to you. I know I've said this a hundred times, but I'll always be there for you. Is there anything I can do?'

'I feel better just talking with you, Jen; sharing the burden and knowing that I can count on you at any time. You and Ben are my props, as Ben would say.'

'That's what besties are for, isn't it? Hey, I've got a little one-year-old here who'd love to hear her godmother— have you got time for a quick chat?'

'Try and stop me,' Sarah smiled.

Hearing Emily's cooing and gurgling reactions to whatever Jennifer was doing with her on the other end of the phone acted as an immediate tonic and she and Jennifer talked for another few minutes about the baby. So that once Sarah pulled up at work she was in a more positive frame of mind. They agreed to continue their conversation that evening.

The day wore on. More often than not managing her consulting projects kept Sarah intensely occupied, demanding absolute focus. However, she was concurrently awaiting client input to most of her ongoing assignments which had created something of a trough in workload, albeit likely to be brief. This afternoon her thoughts malingered and refused to bend to her bidding. She arrived home around six and wasn't due to collect Ben from work until nine. The warmth of the day was diminishing swiftly and the sleeveless dress she'd changed into on reaching her office felt inadequate against the evening chill. She shivered. A few minutes later, after donning leggings and a jumper and making a comforting mug of hot chocolate, Sarah rang Jennifer again.

'Hello, lovely,' Jennifer said brightly. 'Have you got your

hands round a hot choc yet? That's the first thing you need.'

Despite her disquiet, Sarah smiled. 'Ha, you know me so well. Listen, you were asking if there was anything you could do to help. Well, there is, actually.'

'Anything for you.'

'I need to search for Suzette's death certificate online but I'm not sure how to go about it. You've done quite a bit of that sort of investigation—where should I look? Is there a difference between looking at recent records and searching for someone from hundreds of years ago?'

'I used Find My Past and Scotland's People,' Jennifer advised. 'You moved down from Scotland, didn't you? Remind me how old you were when you moved?'

'About one and a half.' As she said those words Sarah put a hand to her mouth. 'God, Dad told me I was nineteen months when my twin died. Perhaps they moved because of it.'

'Maybe they wanted a fresh start,' Jennifer remarked kindly, 'unless they had to move for medical reasons. Maybe your sister was ill. Oh, but you said her death was sudden and unexplained.'

'Do death certificates have the cause of death on them?' Sarah asked quietly. 'I didn't look closely at the ones we found in my parents' attic.'

'Yes, they contain quite a lot of detail, including cause of death and sometimes the duration of any illness which led to the death,' Jennifer responded gently. 'The names of the parents are also recorded, including the mother's maiden name, so it's not difficult to make sure you have the right person. I'd start with the Scottish records, since you know for definite that you were in Ullapool until you were a year and a half old. Would you like me to run a search for you?'

'Thanks Jen, I think I'd like to do it.'

'I understand. Ring me if you have any problems. It's best if you enter as much information as you have. You can specify a range of years when the death might have been registered,' Jennifer added.

'Okay, thanks,' Sarah's voice had reduced to little more than a whisper, almost overcome by anxiety. She was apprehensive about what she might find in the records and, indeed, whether there would be a death record at all. She wanted above all to be able to trust her parents. It still felt almost unthinkable they would lie to her.

'Listen, Sarah,' urged Jennifer, 'I'm here for you no matter what, okay? You know that. You've always been there for me. Jesus, you saved my life. So, whatever this turns out to be, we'll face it together, okay?'

'I know and I appreciate it.' Sarah was acutely aware that, three years ago, Jennifer had spent a good deal of time searching for someone that meant a lot to her and she would understand what it was like to pin all your hopes on the press of a button; the joy of discovering a lost person, the anguish of unearthing terrible news. She realised she needed her friend to be with her on her journey. 'Maybe we could do the search together, while on Skype I mean.'

'Yes, sure. I can talk you through it,' Jennifer replied encouragingly. 'Adam's pottering in the kitchen and keeping an eye on Emily so I have time.'

They logged on Skype via their laptops. Sarah felt comforted by the sight of her friend. As the video connected, Sarah saw Jennifer's generous mouth form a cheerful smile and her emerald eyes sparkle. Her long mahogany hair was fashioned into a plait that fell forward over one shoulder. She was sitting at the dining room table of her old sandstone cottage, framed by a lead-latticed window, partly open. Outside the window Sarah could make out the eager new fronds of a white clematis intertwined with the vigorous stems of a long-established purple wisteria, both in spectacular full flower, and she could imagine their heady perfume.

Sarah shared her screen, launched Scotland's People and they began their search for Suzette.

Jennifer instructed her to begin with the Scottish Statutory Registers. To validate her search, she first interrogated the birth archives and sure enough found the record of Suzette's birth on 20 September 1985, registered in Ullapool. Next, they investigated the deaths in an advanced search. Since Suzette Rose Gregory was an unusual name, Jennifer told Sarah to cast the net widely to encompass the Highlands, setting the time period at 1985 to 1990. There were no matches. They tried using Lester as the surname without success. They tried again, widening the search to the whole of Scotland and a longer period. There were still no matches. They searched using the same area and date criteria with the names Rose Gregory and Rose Lester—again, nothing. There was nothing recorded in the Church Registers of burials either. This implied that the family had moved out of Scotland before Sarah's twin died, which was at odds with what Jake had told her.

Although Sarah believed they had moved directly to Upton-upon-Severn from Ullapool, she began to question her understanding, so she repeated her searches for the whole of England and Wales. There were no records of the death or burial of a Suzette Rose Gregory or Lester from 1985 onwards.

As they concluded the last of the database interrogations, Jennifer developed a look of misgiving that complemented Sarah's incredulity. They were silent for a few moments, each absorbed by individual thoughts.

'They're not being honest with me.' A touch of sadness had perfused Sarah's suspicion.

'It seems that way,' Jennifer responded empathetically. Then, positively, 'so she could still be alive.' Her tone fell again, 'though I'm afraid there could be another explanation.' She took a deeper than usual breath. 'Maybe a body couldn't be produced to enable registration of the death.'

On hearing these words, Sarah was horrified. The thought that something awful may have happened to her sister caused a chill to seep through her body, as though she'd dipped her feet into the icy, deep water of a lake and, in connecting with the darkness, the coldness of the unknown pervaded her entirely. The hairs on her arms rose.

'Oh God... I hadn't thought... I mean I simply accepted she was dead and that it was a kind of cot death. Peaceful.' Her eyes filled with tears.

'It doesn't imply violence,' Jennifer stated hastily. 'What I mean is, perhaps we should consider missing persons. Then maybe we can rule that out.'

Sarah could hear the click of keys being pressed and Jennifer's head was bowed. 'I vaguely recall something about a time period of seven years when there isn't a body,' she sniffed.

'Yes. Here we are,' Jennifer replied, now looking intently at her screen. 'There's a court procedure for declaring a missing person presumed dead. Once a Declaration of Presumed Death has been obtained, then this can be used as evidence of death and a death certificate can be issued. It says here what matters is the strength of evidence that the person has died, rather than the period of time. But if there's insufficient evidence of death then you must show that the person hasn't been known to be alive for at least seven years. Oh, wait a minute… there seems to be a difference between Scotland and England or Wales. Hang on, I'll send you the link.' Jennifer continued reading for a moment or two in silence. Then she said, 'There's text about who can make a Presumption of Death application, or Declarator of Death as it's called in Scotland. In Scotland anyone with an interest can do this but in England only a family member can, not even the police. Interestingly, this website also says the applicant must notify family members and advertise the claim form in the newspapers local to where the missing person lived. So that's something we could check out. But on the other hand, there's no requirement for the family to apply for a declaration of Presumed Death, even if they think the missing person may have died, so no death would be recorded in that case.'

Sarah was processing the information. 'So, as there's no death certificate Suzette's unlikely to have gone missing then been reported presumed dead after seven years,' Sarah voiced her reasoning slowly, separating woven strands of thought. 'We can search newspaper articles about missing persons but in actual fact unless my parents, or someone else, declared her missing, there couldn't be a case for presumed death anyway.' Sarah heaved an exasperated sigh and shook her head. 'If my parents are saying she died—even though that might not be the case—then would they have reported her missing? That seems improbable. It's so confusing; their behaviour is so confusing.'

'All you can do is to take things one step at a time and work through the facts as you find them; you're a good analyst, remember. We'll find a way through the muddle,' promised Jennifer in a reassuring tone. 'Talk to Andy about newspaper records. He's bound to have other ideas too. And I'll have another think.'

Sarah nodded. 'I will, thanks, Jen. I need to talk to Dad again and ask him why there's no death certificate,' she replied, annoyance penetrating her intonation.

'Okay, lovely, we'll speak again soon.'

A distant wail began in the background, gathering strength so that she had to raise her voice over it. 'Love to Adam and my gorgeous howling goddaughter. Take care, bye.'

Sarah shut down her laptop and looked at her watch. It was seven-thirty. Counting on her fingers she calculated the time in Maupiti, assuming her parents were still there, though all the islands were in the same time zone. It would be eight-thirty in the morning. She called Jake's mobile but received no answer. She tried her mother's number, again without success. So, she left a message on her dad's voicemail asking him to call her as soon as possible. She tried to keep an even tone. It wasn't an emergency she said, not wishing to cause alarm, but she needed to talk to him. Frustrated, she turned her attention to making an easy supper of roasted Mediterranean vegetables, which she thought to eat with rice. She was tired, her disturbed night making itself felt. As she chopped and sliced the courgettes, onions and peppers, her knife action became fiercer so that by the time she prepared the aubergine she was slashing at it furiously. She tried her parents' phones every twenty minutes but each time they failed to pick up. Her exasperation at being unable to speak to them added to the myriad emotions churning though her—anger, distress, disillusionment, apprehension—jumbling and merging so that her mind became clogged. She poured herself a large glass of pinot noir and sat at the pine kitchen table staring at the rose-hued stripes in the wood, while her mind was elsewhere. She tried to think sensibly, but her thoughts refused to be controlled, each bleeding into the next with increasing velocity as in a dream, escalating her anxiety. Why were her parent lying? What were they covering up? Did they have something to hide? Was there a terrible incident, maybe a drowning at sea, so there was no body? Or, worse, a drowning at home in the bath that they couldn't bring themselves to report? Had her sister toddled off and not been seen again, declared missing but never presumed dead? Was it their fault she was gone? Did they blame themselves and therefore couldn't tell her? Did they do something illegal? What the hell had happened to Suzette?

Chapter Five

The previous evening, after Sarah apprised Ben of the situation, they talked through all the possibilities they could conceive. At length there appeared to be only three likely explanations: Sarah's parents were not telling the truth and Suzette was known to be alive; Suzette was missing but not officially presumed dead; or Suzette hadn't died in the UK and the record of her death was in the country where she'd died but had not also been registered in the UK.

Sarah knew her parents were lying, though whether Suzette was still alive she had no clue. She would ask her father the moment she managed to get hold of him, but for the time being she had to wait. Since she could do nothing about this first possibility, she determined to investigate the other two options with the help of her friend Andy Finch. An historian at York University, he'd been instrumental in solving a mystery critical to Jennifer's well-being and recovery three years previously and, together with Sarah, had been her principal support at that time. Jennifer and Andy had become close and Sarah had also come to know him as a friend. Jennifer had remembered Andy had an account with the British Library and would easily be able to search old newspaper records. He would also know how to investigate similar databases in other countries. Sarah trusted Andy implicitly; it was a good idea to ask him to help. She had arranged to ring him at lunchtime when they would both have a little time to talk.

At twelve-thirty Sarah hurried to the coffee shop around the corner from the laboratory. The décor was bright yet relaxing and the food—eat-in or take-out—wholesome and reasonably priced. The eatery mainly catered for folk working in the myriad companies that shared the business park and was usually busy. Sarah found a small table at the back of the long room, next to a large castor oil plant that provided a degree of privacy, and ordered a mushroom quiche with salad. She phoned Andy Finch and waited keenly for him to pick up.

'Hi, Sarah! How's my favourite oil girl?'

'Hey there. You don't know any other oil spill scientists,' she laughed.

'Ah, you'd be surprised who I know,' he teased. 'I have my fingers in many pies.'

'Just as long as you're not making a mess of your desk with gravy.'

'Well, I've got something on my jumper but it's not gravy and I haven't actually seen my desk for years,' he kidded, munching something.

Sarah chuckled. She could picture him sitting at his big old, veneered desk, piled high with papers, eating sandwiches pulled from his battered brown briefcase, an untidy little black mongrel with brown eyes at his feet. 'Hope you're sharing your lunch with Scruffy.'

'Ha! He's sharing it with me, more like.'

'How are you, Andy? Still wowing the students with your words of wisdom?'

'Yep, I've still got it. They love me, what can I say? Pity the vice-chancellor doesn't agree,' he chortled. 'Okay, Malvern maiden, hit me with it.'

Sarah giggled. Talking with Andy was always a tonic. She filled him in on the few details he hadn't learned from his brief conversation with Jennifer earlier that morning and confirmed which searches she and Jennifer had already carried out. He then imparted his intelligence.

'I ran a quick search of the British newspaper archives. There are various ways of refining the search, for example within a date range, by country or county, or even by place, and you can search a specific newspaper. But I threw the net wide and searched for mention of a missing person in Scotland between 1950 and 1999. To give you an idea of how comprehensive the database is, this search covered twenty-nine newspapers. I didn't find anything relevant. There were plenty of mentions of missing people but none relating to your circumstances. So I searched for any report that included the name Suzette, Rose, Gregory or Lester. I even tried Suzy, just in case. Then I tried searching all the newspapers in the UK and still drew a blank.'

'Oh… I see.' Sarah frowned. She didn't know how to take this; was it good news or not?

'Sarah, if your twin went missing when she was a baby, it's likely it would have been reported in the press,' Andy advised gently, 'unless it was covered up for some reason, though I can't think why.'

'Right… so there's no record of her death in the UK or of her going missing. Is there any way of finding out whether she went abroad?'

'Well, there are a number of channels we can

investigate,' Andy replied kindly. 'We could look at passport records but they aren't complete. The registers of passport applications in the National Archives only go as far as 1948. Foreign Office passport records have been archived up to 1961 and there are case papers up to 1983, but the more recent records haven't yet been archived. So we'd have to make a written request under the Freedom of Information Act for information on a possible record from 1985 onwards. It'll take twenty working days to get a response.'

Sarah sighed and took a sip of her coffee, which had cooled to lukewarm. 'The thing is, Andy, I don't know why my parents would have taken her abroad.'

'Possibly for some specialist medical treatment,' Andy suggested.

'Hmm, maybe.' Sarah wasn't convinced. 'But if they'd taken her, they surely would have taken me, so I ought to search for my passport record as well.'

'Yes, that's possible,' Andy answered. 'If your parents took you out of the country at that young age you'd have appeared on one of their passports. Your question to the passport office can cover that. But one of your parents could have taken Suzette while the other stayed at home with you. Of course, if someone else took her abroad they may not have used her real name, in which case we have no way of tracing her through a passport record. Your parents told you that she died, didn't they? If she was ill and had to go abroad for treatment, then died abroad, it wouldn't be recorded in the UK statutory registers, unless your folks had specifically applied to register her death with the UK authorities as well as having the death certificate from the country she'd died in; having said that, if they'd brought her body home or had a funeral in the UK they must have registered her death here. And that's not the case, is it?'

'No, we've searched the UK records for a death certificate.' Sarah felt she'd reached another dead end.

'There are other options to consider,' Andy said encouragingly. 'I'm assuming you can't talk with your parents about this?'

'They're currently island hopping in the Pacific and won't engage with me at all; not for the moment anyway. They told me she died in Scotland of something similar to cot death, which clearly isn't the case. So you see what I'm up against. I'm sorry, Andy, to involve you, it's just… I… um… I think there's more to it.'

She took a forkful of quiche, not noticing its warmth had diminished. 'Hmm… so she either died in another country but we don't know which, or she's alive here, or she's alive in another country. But if she did go missing it looks like there was some sort of cover-up.'

'That's about the size of it,' agreed Andy. 'I did look at some other records for you. I searched the Electoral Register for a Suzette Gregory or Lester, also for a Suzy or Rose with those surnames. Again, I came up with nothing. But this could mean several things: if she's alive, she's not in the UK; or she's never been on the Electoral Register, which means she's never voted; or she's using a different name.'

Sarah's thoughts were circling like water towards a plughole. The moment she seemed to grasp the beginnings of an explanation it was swept away again by questions and opposing notions. In letting one theory go to catch another, she had to sift through the evidence again and every supposition needed to be supported. They'd have to eliminate some possibilities.

'Andy, are you able to search foreign records for death certificates?'

'Yes, it can be done. The consular records would be the place to start, assuming that her death was registered at a British consulate. It would help to have some idea of the country. If we're thinking some kind of medical treatment, I could start with the US and maybe Switzerland. It's going to take time though; I've got a lot on and if I don't spend at least a couple of hours a week with Sally she'll be divorcing me. She sees more of Scruffy than me at the moment.'

'I certainly don't want a divorce on my conscience, Doctor Finch,' Sarah smiled. 'Okay, I'm going to speak to Dad, when he actually picks up the bloody phone, and try to get him to talk to me. Thank you so much for all your help. You're a star. Big hugs, give my love to Sally... and Scruffy of course.'

'You're welcome. Let me know if you get anything from your folks. You take care of yourself and give my best to that perfect man of yours. When's he going to make an honest woman of you? He's a keeper.'

'He sure is.'

Sarah waited until nearly seven that evening before ringing her dad once more. Her afternoon had seemed to pass excruciatingly slowly.

When Jake Lester picked up the phone, she felt relieved—she could finally ask the important questions. They spoke for a minute or so about her parents' explorations of Maupiti and Bora Bora; they sounded to be having a wonderful time. Her mother was in the shower, so the call was well-timed from Sarah's perspective. Eventually she took a deep breath and broached the crucial subject.

'Dad, I've been trying to find the death certificate for Suzette online in the UK Registry records but there doesn't appear to be one,' she paused briefly for a response but none came, so she hurried on, 'which I was confused by. I checked the records for Scotland, as that's where you said she'd died, but then I remembered we'd moved about that time, so I looked at the databases for England and Wales, in case...'

'Why d'you need a death certificate?' her father interrupted brusquely, his good humour evaporated. 'Honestly, Sarah, can't you let this lie, at least 'til we return from 'oliday? I've told you where and how she died. What do you want t'go searching fer a certificate fer?'

His abrupt manner halted her for a moment; she wasn't sure how to reply. The previous evening's dreadful thoughts began to engulf her, as water through an open sluice. However, caution chose the words she spoke; she didn't want to accuse her dad outright of lying; she sensed he'd simply clam up. 'Dad, I've been feeling miserable and I wanted to... close the chapter. I've seen Suzette's birth certificate and, somehow, I thought if I could read her death certificate too, I'd be able to move on. I know you don't want to talk about it but I've been anxious, not being able to find it. I mean, why wouldn't there be a death record?'

Jake's tone softened, though Sarah discerned a strange timbre she couldn't identify. 'I see. Well, I expect there's a copy somewhere in the attic. There's no need t' get all het up about it, love. There's probably a simple explanation. Maybe it wurnt digitised—there might've been an error in the archivin' process. The poor little mite died in Scotland and that's all there is to it. It's a long time ago and we've had to move on. And so should you. I know it sounds hard. Now I gotta go. Yer mother's out the shower and we need to get crackin'.'

Sarah doubted a death record could have been overlooked but supposed it was possible. She'd need to check but without a paper copy it would be difficult. She also didn't believe there'd be a copy in her parent's loft; it hadn't been hidden with Suzette's other items and it wasn't in their filing cabinet with all the other important documents. What would be the logic for keeping it elsewhere? She still had so many questions. 'But can I just…'

Jake cut her off. 'We're gonna be off-grid for a while now,' he stated firmly. 'We'll be travellin' between islands and campin' and God knows what the signal'll be like. So don't worry about gettin' hold of us and we won't worry about you. Okay.' The last wasn't a question. 'Big hugs to you and to Ben. Bye, love.'

Sarah barely had time to say goodbye before her father rang off and was left feeling upset and, oddly, slightly bereft, although she couldn't have explained why.

By eight pm she'd decided on a course of action and had booked the rest of the week off work. She would be going to Ullapool.

Chapter Six

Ullapool, Scotland, 10 May 2018

Sarah and Ben arrived in Ullapool mid-afternoon that Thursday, having caught a flight from Birmingham to Inverness, where they hired a car for the last 60 miles of the 530-mile journey from Malvern. It was a bright warm day although a persistent breeze ruffled the surface of the Moray Firth, creating a ribbed blue-grey carpet of ripples.

They drove north-west, mountains rising around them. The sun glinted off the surface of Loch Garve as they passed by, driving through dappled shadows formed by the burgeoning hillside trees celebrating spring and sifting the sunlight. Beneath the canopy, rich green mosses blanketing rocky outcrops intermingled with toffee-brown bracken, last year's desiccated growth spread protectively over precious new shoots. Further on, Sarah and Ben travelled through dense green coniferous forest and over brown scrubby moorland, broken only by an occasional patch of stubby grass pasture where windswept highland cattle grazed. After about an hour they pulled off the road to sit on a pebble beach at the edge of Loch Glascarnoch, sharing a Scotch pie, oatcakes and cheese. Massive rocky heather-strewn hills rose before and behind them and, in the distance, the snow-capped peaks of Beinn Dearg ascended magnificently skyward.

On reaching the little town of Ullapool they headed for the harbour where a handful of sailing boats were moored in the loch and a few fishing vessels clung to one side of a double pier. On the other pier was a modest ferry terminal serving passengers to and from the Outer Hebrides. The houses along the seafront were mainly pretty, whitewashed terraced cottages, some converted to cafés and shops, several of which offered woollens and gifts. They found a car park tucked between two residential back streets decorated with pink cherry trees in blossom. A helpful woman in a thick coat directed them to the tourist information centre, opposite an art gallery and next to a delectable delicatessen on a street behind the harbour.

They had discussed what the best approach might be and decided to find an old established business, perhaps family-run, whose owners had lived there in the mid-1980s. Researching the town's history during their journey north, Sarah discovered it had once been a bustling fishing port, though not much larger than the current settlement. She knew her father had run a small shop selling outdoor activity gear, a fact that might be of some help in her quest to locate someone who used to know her parents.

The woman at the tourist information centre was obliging. She appeared to be somewhere in her late fifties and told them she'd moved to Ullapool in the early 1990s and didn't know anyone called Lester. However, she was pretty sure the outdoor shop had been run by the same family for a while and that they might have bought the business as far back as the '80s, although she thought the store had changed location since that time. She also suggested trying the harbour office, since the current harbourmaster's father had been harbourmaster before him and had lived in Ullapool all his life.

Optimistic, Sarah and Ben set off for the shop first, which was a short way down the road. It was a well-stocked store and had a welcoming café. They ordered two cappuccinos and asked if they could speak with the owner. A red-haired man in his early fifties with a long bushy beard came to talk with them. Sarah showed him an old photo of her parents and herself sitting on the quayside in Upton, taken when she was about six. It had been shot from a close range and all three of them were nicely in focus. Lena was clad in colourful loose-fitting trousers and a flowery cotton top whilst Jake sported baggy khaki shorts and a black T-shirt with a checked shirt tied around his waist. Sarah, dressed in blue dungarees, was sitting on her mother's lap and the three of them were laughing at something. Sarah smiled at the photo as she handed it to the proprietor.

'That's Dad in his grunge phase,' she said.

The man studied the photo for a moment and shook his head. 'Sorry, ah canna help ye. We bought this business in the late '90s and it wasnae from a man called Lester ah'm afraid. The guy we bought it from moved away. Ah dinnae ken where he went,' he said regretfully.

'Ah, okay. Well, thanks for your time,' Sarah replied disappointedly. 'Nice coffee by the way.'

Outside the shop Ben took her hand. 'Come on,' he said brightly, 'next stop the harbourmaster.'

It wasn't hard to find the harbour office, which was located on the pier close to the ferry terminal. They entered and asked a youngish man if they could speak with the harbourmaster. The man informed them that his chief had been on the phone, but he would check whether he was now available. He disappeared through a door for a few moments and came back with a tall, neatly dressed fellow in slacks and a blue short-sleeved cotton shirt. The man's brown eyes sparkled in his weather-beaten face as he smiled at Ben and Sarah. 'Hello there,' he said in a deep voice. 'How can ah help ye nice folk?'

Sarah explained she was looking for someone who'd known her parents and gave him the photo.

He looked at it and grinned. 'Is that you? You were a bonnie bairn. Lester, ye say?' For a few moments he frowned and tapped his lips with a finger, concentrating, as if trying to haul a long-forgotten memory from deep within his mind. 'Aye, ah ken their faces well enough. Ah'm trying t'remember why. Ah would ha' been around ten when yer folk were here.'

'We understand that your father used to be the harbourmaster here. If someone ran a shop selling fishing gear and suchlike, perhaps he would have known them,' Ben said hopefully.

'Aye, perhaps, but ye hae to remember that Ullapool wus a busy auld place in thae days. No' only were there many more fishing vessels than today, but there wus a whole fleet o' large factory ships from Russia and East Germany an' the like anchored in the loch, processing mackerel. Then there were all the ferries servicing the ships an' the businesses supplying hundreds o' folk. It wus a thriving place an' no mistake. Kept ma da on his toes, ah can tell ye.' As Sarah's face dropped, he added, 'Dinnae worry though, ma auld mam will recollect; sure to. She pretty much knows everyone who's lived here for more than a few years. She'll blether to anyone, bless her.'

'Do your parents still live here?' Sarah asked expectantly.

'Aye. Been in the same hoose for over fifty years. Come tae think o' it, yer folk could ha' been neighbours.' He nodded slowly, as his recollection intensified. 'Aye, that's mebbie where I ken them from.'

'Really?' asked Sarah excitedly. She squeezed Ben's hand.

'Ah'll introduce ye to Mam,' the harbourmaster stated decisively. He looked at his watch. It was nearly five. 'Just give me a couple o' minutes.'

'Wonderful,' Sarah replied.

'Thank you,' added Ben.

'Ah'm Douglas by the way.' He held out a hand. Sarah and Ben introduced themselves.

Douglas called to the young man, asking him to hold the fort. 'Craig'll be here in a wee while and ah'm on the mobile.' He grinned at Ben and Sarah, inclining his head towards his assistant. 'The laddie's learning the ropes. He's a bright lad. Ma next-in-command's shift starts in fifteen minutes, so we can get going noo.'

Ben and Sarah followed Douglas as he walked out onto the coastal road and turned left past the ferry port entrance. They had to walk quickly to match his pace as he strode along the seafront. The breeze had subsided and the westerly sun, peaceful in its late afternoon phase, cast a golden light magnanimously over the little town. They proceeded along West Shore Street, passing a long row of terrace houses of varying sizes, some faced with stone but most painted white. The sea loch to their left was calm and inviting, its light blue reflecting a clear sky. Rolling hills either side of the loch stretched into the distance, bathing in the water.

'It's a lovely spot,' Ben remarked. 'The view from these houses is superb.'

'Aye, so it is,' answered Douglas. 'Ye can see why ma parents dinnae wanna move. These plots hae reasonably big gardens so when the bairns came along—that's me an' ma wee sister—they simply extended out the back. Ma folk are up there, near the point.'

When they had almost reached the tip of the headland Douglas knocked at the door of a double-fronted, rendered cottage, before opening it and announcing himself. A plump lady of about seventy with reddish-brown curly hair and the same sparkly eyes as her son came into the hallway. 'Ah, Dougie, yer just in time fer a cuppa,' she beamed as he gave her a hug. 'An' who are these young folk?' she added amiably.

'This is Sarah an' this is Ben,' he replied. 'Folks, this is ma mam, Moira. Mam, they're wanting to speak with someone who may have known Sarah's parents when they lived here in the '80s. Ah thought you might be able t' help.'

'Come in, come in,' Moira beckoned welcomingly. 'Athair's in the sitting room,' she informed her son. 'I'll make a pot an' join you.'

They entered a long bright room with windows front and back. The walls were painted apple white and covered with wooden-framed photos portraying various dogs and what looked like a large family. A slim grey-haired man with bushy eyebrows was sitting in an armchair watching the television. He seemed a good ten years older than his wife. His craggy features conveyed a familiarity with the elements, expressing a life contiguous with the ocean. Douglas introduced his father to Ben and Sarah as Alastair and explained the purpose of their visit to him. Alastair turned off the television, indicating they should take a seat on the sofa. As soon as he heard the name Lester he nodded. 'Och aye, that name's familiar.'

Sarah handed him her photo.

'Aye, that's them alright. They lived right next door.' He pointed through the wall. 'Braw couple, though it wus a strange business, them flitting an' no' saying goodbye. Màthair will remember.'

At that moment Moira came in with a full tray and proceeded to set out teacups, saucers and a plate of shortbread biscuits on a low wooden table between two armchairs. Once the tea had been poured and the shortbread distributed the conversation turned again to the Lesters.

'Is that you, Sarah?' Moira said, not expecting a reply. 'Och, you always were bonnie wee lasses, both you an' your sister. Take after yer màthair; she wus a braw lass too.'

'You knew my sister?' Sarah's heart was thumping.

'Course we did,' replied Moira, surprised. 'Ma lassie Iona—that's Dougie's sister—used to play with ye an' yer sister in the garden. You're aw aboot the same age. I dinnae suppose ye remember.'

Sarah reached into an inside jacket pocket to retrieve a second photo, which she handed to Moira. 'That's the earliest picture of me I could find. I think it must have been taken here. I don't have a photo of Suzette.'

'Och, look at ye in yer wee blae trews!' Moira chuckled, as she passed the picture to her husband. 'Wull ye look at that, Alastair.' She rose from her chair and walked towards the door. 'Wait a minute.'

Sarah turned her attention to the elderly man. 'You said something about a strange business when they moved. Do you remember what happened? Did something happen to me or my sister?'

'No' that ah recall but then ah didnae see that much o' ye. Moira and yer màthair, weel, they were verra close fer a while. Moira was upset when yer parents upped an' flitted suddenly wi'oot a word.'

Sarah wanted to make sure she fully understood. 'So my mum and your wife were good friends, but Mum left without saying anything and you've not heard from her since?'

'That's aboot the size o' it,' Alastair concurred.

'And my sister and I were both... well... when they, I mean we, moved?' Sarah continued guardedly.

The old man shrugged. 'Ah assume sae, I dinnae ken. Best tae ask Màthair, she'll be back in a minute.'

Sarah glanced at Ben as she sipped her tea, waiting for Moira to return. He wore a quizzical expression. 'Maybe they moved to somewhere else in Scotland before Upton,' he suggested quietly.

Sarah's jumbled thoughts were abruptly interrupted by Douglas asking where they were staying the night.

'We've booked a B and B just north of Ullapool. It's on a hill, somewhere called Ardmair. Looks like it's got beautiful views towards the Summer Isles,' Ben replied cheerily.

Moira reappeared, waving a large photo album decorated with pictures of roses. 'Ah knew ah'd find it,' she declared, pleased with herself. She indicated to Douglas to take her armchair and squeezed herself between Sarah and Ben on the sofa, opening the book near the beginning. 'There ye are,' she pointed.

Ben and Sarah followed her finger. The picture had been taken on a sunny day. Two identical blonde toddlers, both in blue trousers, one in a red jumper, the other in a pink one, were sitting on a large tartan blanket with a little brown-haired girl of about the same age, playing with colourful wooden blocks. All three children were concentrating on the blocks in their little hands and next to them was a jumbled pile of the same wooden bricks which looked as if a previously-constructed wall had recently tumbled.

Sarah gasped. She felt herself reeling from successive shocks, as if standing in the shallows of the ocean being pounded by breakers—she and Suzette were identical... conceived from one fertilised egg... with the same genes; they looked indistinguishable then and would today if Suzette was alive. She tried to absorb and process the fact, wondering why the thought hadn't crossed her mind before. In the photo she had of herself she was also wearing those blue trousers and red jumper and was sitting, alone, on the same tartan rug in the same garden. A sudden sense of profound loss overwhelmed her, a sensation that she was no longer whole.

Moira was smiling, as if recollecting a happy day. 'Yer mum took that and gave me a copy. We had some nice times. How are yer mum and dad and how's Suzy? We havnae heard from them since they left.'

Sarah looked at Ben for some indication of what to say. Her mind was in a daze.

Ben spoke gently for her. 'I'm afraid Sarah doesn't

remember Suzette. You see we understand that unfortunately she died before she was two.'

Moira put her hands to her mouth. 'Och no,' she cried, 'Ah'm so verra sorry. Och, that's terrible; yer poor parents, an' poor you, Sarah.'

'The thing is,' Ben continued softly, 'Sarah only discovered she had a twin a few days ago. Her folk are away and we're trying to find out about Suzette and how she died. Sarah was brought up in Worcestershire, but we believe her twin died in Scotland before her parents moved. So we wondered if you might know something about that. But clearly you didn't know; we're sorry to have brought bad news.'

'Màthair, do ye ken whether both girls were well around the time the Lesters went?' Alastair asked.

'Aye, ye were both in good health. Yer mum and I took ye all to play on the beach the day before ye left,' Moira replied, addressing Sarah. 'Ah'm sorry for yer loss, lass, but Suzy didnae die in Ullapool or we'd hae kent aboot it. It was strange the way yer folks left suddenly. We'd been making plans fer Easter—ah recall it wus late that year an' we were hoping for a bit o' warmer weather—an' then the next day ye were gone. Something else wus a bit odd,' she continued, glancing at her husband. 'Aboot a week afterwards a foreign lad came to the door asking after yer parents. Said he was a friend trying to find them. O' course, we didnae ken where they were. The reason ah recall is because when ah told Alastair he mentioned that a foreign man had been asking after them a couple o' weeks before, but when ah described the man who came to the hoose it wisnae the same lad an' we thought that wus a bit peculiar. O' course, there were a lot o' men from abroad around in thae days but somehoo their accents didnae fit.'

On hearing this Sarah nodded her head almost imperceptibly. Her heart was now pounding so hard she felt they could all hear it. She tried to keep her voice steady to avoid betraying her anxiety. 'These foreign men, do you recall what they looked like or what kind of accents they had?'

Moira and Alastair looked at one another. Moira shook her head and Alastair pulled his mouth into a shrug. 'Sorry lass, it wus a long time ago,' responded Moira.

'Ah dinnae think they were East European,' returned Alastair, frowning slightly. 'There were a lot o' thae around at that time. Ah only recollect the man that spoke to me being different.'

'Aye,' agreed Moira, 'no Russian or German'.

'Alastair, were all the visitors to Ullapool who arrived by sea subject to a passport check in the '80s?' asked Ben, evidently trying a different tack. 'You said there were a lot of foreigners around; presumably all the boats had to register with your office?'

'Aye, lad, all the boats widae been registered and we did look at identification. Boats had tae radio ahead before coming into the harbour. But there were hundreds o' folk on factory ships in the loch in thae days; most stayed aboard but no' all. It wud no' hae been verra difficult tae come ashore off one o' thae vessels withoot an inspection.'

'I see,' rejoined Ben, 'so if someone was around and up to no good they couldn't have simply sailed in and anchored in the harbour without checking in at the harbourmaster's office.'

'Ah ran a tight ship,' Alastair confirmed seriously, 'all vessels were recorded. Ye hae tae remember, that wus the time o' the cold war and Ullapool wus a major destination fer the klondykers. But that's no' tae say that security in all the ports along this coast wus sae strict. Holidaymakers wud hae been able tae sail around withoot personal identification checks in many places.'

'Are ye thinking that thae foreign men who asked after the Lesters were up tae no good?' asked Moira, slightly shocked.

'We don't know,' Ben shook his head sadly. 'We're just trying to piece information together.'

Sarah stood abruptly and nodded first to Moira then to her husband and finally to Douglas. 'I think we've taken up enough of your time,' she said matter-of-factly. 'Thank you all so much for your help. It's been a pleasure to meet you, it truly has. I'm sorry we brought bad news.' She cast Ben an almost imperceptible head tilt in the direction of the door. She needed to be out of the company of strangers.

Ben stood too and shook hands with their hosts. 'It's been useful talking with you and lovely to meet you.'

'Wull ye take this photo?' Moira held out the picture of the three children playing.

Sarah was taken aback. 'Oh, I couldn't. They're your memories. But thank you for your kindness.' She turned and walked quickly past Ben to the front door, obliging him to step back to let her pass.

Moira tapped Ben on the arm and quietly offered him the photo. 'Yer lass said she doesn't hae a photo o' Suzy. Go on, take it. Ye can give it back one day, when ye hae another o' the lassie. That way we'll see ye again.'

Ben smiled and gave her a peck on one cheek. 'You're so kind,' he said, accepting it. 'We'll definitely return it to you; that's a promise.'

Douglas held out a business card. 'You can get in touch via me,' he stated warmly. 'Good luck. Ah hope ye find some peace.'

By the time Ben reached the front door Sarah was standing across the road with her back to the house, staring out across the loch. His thoughts had turned darkly to kidnap or worse. It might follow that a foreigner committing an illegal act could have arrived or escaped by boat. He could have committed an appalling crime but Ben chose not to dwell on murder and quickly dismissed that unspeakable theory. He walked to Sarah's side and put an arm around her shoulders. As he touched her, she turned her face into his chest and sobbed.

Ben held her tightly against him, stroking her hair. The great tenderness he felt for her welled, constricting his throat and threatening to overspill. His features resisted, choosing a determined guise, and his mood followed suit. He became angry against the unseen and unknown; those who would lie to his precious girl about her sister and seek to harm her and tear her family apart. He vowed to himself he would get to the bottom of whatever this was. As soon as Jake and Lena returned, he would speak with them in private and demand they be candid with him. Whatever they'd said to shield their daughter—he had no doubt now they were lying, maybe to protect her but, more likely, themselves—it was time for the truth. She deserved their honesty and had a right to know. From the moment he'd been introduced to them, they'd welcomed him into their family. They'd provided a vital missing component in his life and gradually he'd allowed himself to trust and love them. Now, like Sarah, he felt betrayed.

Eventually Sarah's tears subsided and she turned her face towards him. He tenderly kissed each moist cheek and the tip of her nose before kissing her gently on the lips. 'C'mon,' he said, leading her across the grass in front of them and down onto a narrow shingle beach. They sat for some time, he with his arm around her, gazing over the silver-blue water towards the inner sanctuary of Loch Broom, each lost in their thoughts.

At length it was Sarah who broke the silence. 'What the fuck is going on? Mum and Dad are lying to me—they've never done that before—they don't tell me I had a twin sister then they tell me she's dead and died at home in Scotland; they told me they moved from Ullapool to Upton but Suzette clearly didn't die in Ullapool; Mum had a close friend here but they disappeared without saying goodbye to her; there are two foreign men asking where my parents are. And there's no death certificate for Suzette!' She picked up a pebble and threw it angrily at the water.

'Nothing makes sense right now but we'll bloody well uncover it,' answered Ben doggedly. He gave her a hug and took her left hand in his. 'There's one thing I'm certain of,' he continued resolutely, 'your parents love you, more than anything else in the world. I could see it in their eyes the moment I met them and, believe me, that's more important than any of this; take it from one who never had any parents.'

'I just wish they'd been honest with me when I was old enough to know. I mean, whatever happened, surely they could have shared it with me. At the least they could be frank with me now.'

'Perhaps they did have to go out of the country suddenly for some reason and Suzette died abroad,' Ben shrugged. 'Perhaps that's why there were foreigners asking after them,' he continued unconvincingly.

Sarah shook her head, echoing his thoughts. 'What if Suzette was kidnapped? Oh God, I can hardly bear to think about it,' her voice had reduced to a rasp. 'I mean, anything could have…'

Ben interrupted to save her from having to say the dreaded word. He spoke evenly, 'If she was kidnapped or murdered it's likely it would've been in the newspapers but it wasn't. So let's not think the worst.' He squeezed her hand. There was nothing to be gained by picturing the direst scenario. Although he suspected foul play, it seemed to him likely Lena and Jake must have somehow been involved or, at least, have been aware of some illegal activity, and he couldn't possibly imagine them being implicated in such a terrible crime.

Sarah held her head in her hands for several long moments. Then, looking up into the distance, she said slowly, 'This is a deliberate cover up. I know it. Do you think maybe Suzette's death was in some way Mum and Dad's fault? Maybe it was an accident, but they were somehow negligent and someone, a foreigner, found out and tried to blackmail them? Perhaps they covered it up and maybe there was no body, which is why there's no death certificate, and they had to move suddenly.'

'Hmm, I guess that could make sense. It would explain why there were no newspaper reports and why there were people asking about them,' Ben agreed. He'd been considering other possibilities. 'But we still don't know for certain that she did die. You know we could check with the police.'

Sarah grabbed a handful of white pebbles, letting them fall gradually though her fingers, while she contemplated Ben's suggestion. 'I'd rather not involve the police, not yet anyway. To say I'm angry at my parents is an understatement, but we don't know what we're getting into here and I… I don't want to get them into trouble; we're not yet aware of all the facts.'

Ben nodded his understanding of her reticence.

Sarah lowered her head again. 'You know, maybe someone did take her and my parents knew who it was and either couldn't, or didn't want to, stop them. Christ, anything could have happened to her.'

Ben rose to his feet. 'C'mon,' he said positively, offering a hand to help her up, 'we're going around in emotional circles when we should be approaching this methodically. Let's go and have a pint and get something to eat. We've had a long day, I'm starving and we've still got to find the B and B.'

'Okay. I'll try and hang on to a bit of logic but it's fast disappearing,' Sarah responded wryly, clambering up off the shingle. 'A pint would be great though.'

Chapter Seven

Malvern, England, 15 May 2018

The following Tuesday evening, Sarah received a call from Andy Finch. She sat at the kitchen table to talk with him, pouring herself a glass of Shiraz from a half empty bottle.

'Hi Malvern maid, how're you doing? Found any other secret trunks in attics?' he said brightly.

'No more trunks but plenty of secrets,' she replied, trying, but failing, to summon a little cheer to match his.

'You want to tell me? Anything that might help our quest?' his tone thoughtful now, befitting her disposition. She noted he'd said 'our quest' and found it comforting.

'You first.' She was eager for any scrap of information he may have uncovered.

'Well, I'm afraid I don't have much to offer at this stage. I made a formal request under the Freedom of Information Act to the National Archives for any passport record in the name of Suzette Gregory or Suzette Lester. We now must wait around twenty days for their response—it could take longer. I also searched the US and Swiss consular records and haven't found any death certificates. But that's not surprising. I mean the world is a big place. We're fishing in the dark without knowing where to drop the hook.'

He was clearly trying to manage her expectations. Sarah told him of their visit to Ullapool and suspicions of kidnap or blackmail and of her parents' possible involvement or, at least, knowledge of what took place and the fact that they lied to her.

It was some moments before Andy replied and the silence seemed interminable. Sarah knew he'd be thinking over what she'd told him, sifting the information and deciding which strand to follow. Even so, she wondered if he was now regretting being involved. As she was dismissing that last thought, he responded, pensively.

'Well, that's quite a turn of events. Obviously if Suzette was kidnapped, and possibly died, there wouldn't be a registration of death at the time, regardless of whether it was in the UK or abroad. But the fact that no one reported her "missing presumed dead" after seven years implies your parents had a reason for not doing so. Perhaps they hoped she was alive and didn't want her death to be formally assumed, or, as unthinkable as it is, they were connected somehow. I'm sorry to re-emphasise this, I mean you know it already, but if a loved one goes missing it's usually reported within twenty-four hours, sooner if it's a child.'

Sarah bowed her head, supporting her forehead in her hand, her elbow on the table. By now she was certain her parents must have been embroiled somehow in her sister's disappearance or death; Ben thought so too. But hearing it from Andy triggered surges of anxiety which heaved and welled from deep inside, causing her hands to shake and her legs to tremble. She sat up, feeling slightly dizzy, and took a gulp of wine then registered Andy's voice as if from a distance. He was asking if she was alright.

'Yeah, sorry, just processing. Christ!'

'Look,' he continued evenly, 'your folks haven't reported Suzette missing or dead and it's clear they're lying to you about her having died in Ullapool, so if she was kidnapped, or taken with their knowledge, then she could well be alive somewhere.' A hint of optimism infiltrated his tone. 'Just because we haven't found her yet doesn't mean we won't.'

Amid the enveloping shadows, Sarah found herself clinging onto one crucial word. 'Yes, of course, she could be alive. There's no actual evidence that she died, is there?'

'No. So, we can see what the passport search brings and go from there. I'm assuming you don't want to ask the police at this stage.'

'No, I can't. I…'

'And you're going to confront your mum and dad when they get back,' Andy stated, evidently not expecting a response.

'Yeah, for sure. But they're currently avoiding me. Last time we spoke, Dad used his "the matter is closed" voice and said they'd probably be difficult to get hold of. They've not answered my calls for days. It's weeks until they come home. I'm not holding out hope they'll open up when they're back, especially if they're mixed up in something.'

'Okay. Bear in mind that if Suzette was taken and has grown up somewhere else, her name is likely to have been changed.'

'So, we'll have no idea what her name would be, therefore can't search any records and won't know where to start,' Sarah exclaimed.

'That's about the size of it. But at least we know what she'd look like.'

Chapter Eight

Ten days later, Ben phoned Sarah, mid-morning at work, to cancel their prearranged lunch to fit in an additional swim coaching session to cover for a colleague who was ill. Sarah decided to treat herself anyway, since she rarely had time for a full lunch break, and would make the most of the opportunity today. The bright midday sun had bleached the sky, rendering it almost indistinguishable from the diaphanous traces of wispy cloud which lingered motionless, high above the old, terraced shops in Great Malvern. She needed to buy birthday cards, so called into a stationery store before heading towards the café she'd thought to try. Her phone pinged as she was exiting with her purchases and she stood to one side of the pavement to check the messages, her back warming in the sun as she shielded the screen from its glare.

Suddenly another shadow appeared and a voice uttered, '*Suzette? Que fais-tu ici? Es-tu venu avec Xavier?*'

Sarah whipped around to face a stylishly dressed woman with dark, grey-streaked hair. 'I'm sorry, what did you say?' she replied, incredulous. Her heart pounded in her chest.

The woman took a step backwards, her eyes widening as the recognition of her mistake spread across her features. She raised a manicured hand as if to deflect any advancement from Sarah. 'Oh, I'm so sorry, I mistook you for someone else. Apologies.' She turned to go.

'Wait a minute,' exclaimed Sarah. 'Did you call me Suzette?'

The stranger spoke quickly. 'An error on my part,' she responded in a clipped tone. 'I'm sorry for disturbing you.' She began to walk quickly away.

Astonishment had rooted Sarah to the spot momentarily but as soon as the woman crossed the road she sprang into action and ran after her, having to dodge two cars and a bicycle in the process.

'Stop, please. I'm looking for someone called Suzette who looks like me. She's my twin sister. Do you know her?' she cried.

A hint of irritation infected the woman's intonation. 'I told you I was mistaken. My friend's name is Soubrette and you don't look like her. I saw you from the back and made a mistake. I'm sorry. I don't know your sister. Now excuse me, I must go.' She walked briskly away.

For a few moments, Sarah was impeded by the woman's denial. Her thoughts were like her mouth after a spoonful of peanut butter. Then, as she digested the woman's words, filaments of comprehension crystallised. She was sure the woman had called her Suzette. Someone who looks like her with the name Suzette could not possibly be a coincidence.

'She's alive. My God, she's alive,' she whispered in amazement; she could hardly believe it and needed to say it out loud, to ground the fact, here and now, in reality. Exhilaration and relief flooded her senses. She closed her eyes for a few moments, overwhelmed. Then, still reeling with shock, she cast around for the stranger. Spotting her at twenty yards or so she followed, removing her noticeable red jacket and tying it around her waist inside out.

Sarah hung back as the woman entered and exited several shops, making her way up the steep hill onto the high street, though she didn't seem to be carrying shopping. She disappeared into an eatery inhabiting an old Regency building nestled against the steep rise leading onto Sugarloaf Hill and the Worcestershire Beacon. Nervous of being seen, Sarah cautiously approached the entrance moments later and peeked inside around the door frame. For a second it crossed her mind how odd she must look. The room stretched back a long way and expanded to the left beyond a long wooden bar. The woman was being directed to a table in the area out of view. Sarah waited until she'd gone before entering. Passing some large comfortable leather sofas, she selected a small pine table set against the wall in one of the many cosy alcoves at the rear, around the corner from where she'd seen the woman heading.

The rooms were filling quickly with chatter. From where she was sitting, Sarah had a limited view of other tables. Some folk were on their lunch break, two men engaged in a business discussion, whilst a group of four pensioners clearly intended a more leisurely repast complete with bottles of wine. Trepidation had quashed her appetite. She looked at the menu for something light and quick to prepare—she wasn't sure how long she'd be staying—and chose a pan-fried fillet of sea bass. When it arrived, she was too agitated to enjoy it properly but picked at it, pushing the accompanying crushed herb potatoes around her plate. She frequently glanced up surreptitiously, checking for signs of her quarry. A peculiar mixture of relief and anger overcame her senses and it was all she could do to keep from bursting into tears. She was brought sharply into focus by the presence of a waiter who appeared to be asking her how her food was. She answered politely that it was delicious while pushing her plate away, apologising for her lack of appetite, and ordered a coffee. She tried to recall exactly what the woman had said, but all she could hear was 'Suzette'. Had she misheard? Had she wanted so much to hear that name she was the one who'd been mistaken? Soubrette, Suzette; she repeated the names under her breath, apprehension and uncertainty joining her emotional turmoil.

While sipping her cappuccino she heard the ringing of a phone nearby. It was clearly not good news for then came a loud male voice speaking angrily and quickly in a foreign language.

'*Ils ne peuvent pas faire ça! Putain!*'

As the man dropped his voice and continued his exasperating conversation a surge of adrenalin swept through Sarah's body and her heart raced. The walls of the room began to spin and her vision narrowed until everything grew dark and all she could see was the brown and white coffee cup in her trembling hands. The cup disappeared and was replaced by the impression of a man's face. Everything was in slow motion. The image, blurred at first, grew clearer. His dark brown hair framed clean-shaven, defined cheekbones, a long straight nose and brown eyes. As the face came into focus, a long high sound rang in Sarah's ears, becoming louder and louder. She dropped the cup from her quaking fingers and put her hands over her ears. She tried to block the man's face from her vision by shutting her eyes but it refused to go. '*Putain,*' it mouthed, '*putain!*'

An elderly lady sitting at a nearby table walked over and placed her hand gently on Sarah's arm. 'Are you alright, dear?'

The touch was enough to bring her back to her senses and the room assumed its former shape and colour as if nothing had happened. But something certainly had happened.

Sarah was shaking. An unexplained feeling of dread had overcome her. It pulled at her stomach and wrapped around her chest, constricting her lungs. She tried to stand, grabbing at the table to steady herself as her knees wouldn't support her.

'You look as though you've had a shock. Would you like another coffee?' The elderly lady didn't wait for an answer but proceeded to the bar to order a drink.

Sarah slowly righted the coffee cup in front of her and mopped the table with a tissue from her pocket. She leaned her elbows on the surface and rested her head in her hands, trying to make sense of what had happened. Her heart was still beating wildly and she took deep breaths to try to calm it. It was the voice: that word. She knew that voice, yet couldn't place it. It belonged to the face, the features of someone she did not know. Yet both the face and voice had triggered a genuine fear within her. Intuition told her this had to be connected with the woman who'd mistaken her. She felt flushed and badly wanted fresh air. She needed to set eyes on the man to whom the voice belonged, but she had an intense instinct that she should not allow him to see her and knew herself well enough to heed that.

Sarah rose slowly from her seat as the elderly lady returned to their alcove. 'Thank you. You're very kind. I'm alright now. I just need some fresh air.'

The lady offered her the cup of coffee she'd purchased.

'Thank you but no. Please, you have it. Thanks for your concern.'

Sarah was still shaking as she walked quickly to the bar to settle her bill, keeping her back turned on the area from where the voice had come and where the woman she'd followed was presumably seated. She exited the restaurant, crossed the road and proceeded down a short flight of stone steps onto a shaded terrace. She walked along the terrace under two large London plane trees, past masses of faded red and white tulips, and sat on a bench amongst the bright magenta flowers and red stems of a multitude of elephant ears. Although some way away, she had a clear view of the entrance to the bistro that would not be obvious to a person leaving it. The terrace was a little green haven in the middle of the busy intersection of three roads, but Sarah's focus was on the blue doorway and she waited nervously.

The woman appeared first, scanning the street and donning sunglasses as she stepped into the sunshine. Subsequently a tall, well-groomed man emerged and they lingered briefly near the entrance, exchanging a few words before parting. Sarah gasped involuntarily. His face was unmistakably the same as that which had manifested uninvited in her consciousness fifteen minutes earlier. He had a short dark-grey beard but there was no doubt in her mind this was the same man. Her palms began to sweat. She closed her eyes briefly and saw an image of him as before. This time she seemed to be viewing him from slightly further away. Some sort of bundle obscured his chest and arms as he stared at her unnervingly.

She opened her eyes and gathered herself quickly. The man was heading in her direction, albeit on the pavement a little way above the terrace where she was sitting. The woman had proceeded the opposite way and was obscured temporarily by traffic. Sarah panicked; who should she be concerned with—the woman who seemed to know her sister or the man who'd provoked such an alarming reaction? Were these strangers connected with the disappearance of her twin? As he came closer her choice was removed; she could no longer see the woman and could not yet make a move. She bent to collect her bag from underneath the bench as he drew nearer, keeping her head down until she could be sure he had passed by. Then she stood for a few seconds, considering what she was about to do. She was normally level-headed and logical. Yet he was associated with the woman and she with Suzette, so her compulsion was to follow him, to find out more, even though she felt inexplicably afraid of him.

Chapter Nine

Sarah ran back along the terrace, up the steps and across the road. Her target was some way off now but being tall and slim and dressed in a dark blue suit she could still distinguish him. He crossed over the road at the top of Church Street and headed down Edith Walk to the car park. Sarah kept her distance as she watched him climb into a smart black Jaguar XJ and noted the registration number. It was a popular parking location and her own car was parked nearby. He drove onto a main road leading to Malvern Link Common and continued across the parkland. Sarah was familiar with the route as she often drove this way on her journey back to work from the town centre. She found herself following the Jaguar right into the industrial estate on the edge of town where her company was located. He pulled into a small car park in front of a pharmaceutical company's building. Sarah continued until she could turn her car around and park on the opposite side of the road. She took a deep breath and wondered what to do next.

Where had she seen him before? Why did he frighten her? She closed her eyes to concentrate on his face and the word he had spoken. When she thought of him speaking that word the same image appeared. He was staring at her with wild dark eyes and in his arms was a bundle. A horrible wail resounded inside her head then the image changed. She was seeing her own face as a baby, as captured in her mother's photos, except there was something not quite right with her face, something different.

Sarah opened her eyes, let go of the breath she'd been holding and tried to calm herself. She felt slightly nauseous for a few moments. Once that passed and her heart stopped thumping, she was left with an odd feeling of desolation. She considered the dreadful howling sound and realised it was somehow connected with the despair and loss she sensed. Having experienced a vivid image of the stranger looking younger and without a beard implied to her it had to be a memory, rather than a fictional image conjured up by hearing his voice and that his voice and the sight of him had triggered that memory emerging out of her subconscious. Anger joined her mix of emotions again; anger at the stranger who'd activated such a bizarre emotive response and at the woman who'd spoken the name Suzette then denied knowing her. A wave of dread swept through her body, coming to lie heavy in the pit of her stomach. The baby she'd seen in her mind's eye wasn't her: it was Suzette.

She resolved to act but wasn't sure what to do. She retrieved her phone from the bag on the seat, dialled her laboratory and told a colleague she didn't feel well and wouldn't be working the rest of the day. As she replaced the phone in her bag her fingers touched nail scissors, giving her an idea.

Sarah donned Ben's old baseball cap, fortuitously left on the back seat, as a precaution against being recognised and climbed out of her Toyota. She crossed the road and entered the car park, looking for security cameras. There didn't appear to be any. The area was full of vehicles, nevertheless it was quiet as staff had already returned to work. She strode quickly to the black Jaguar and crouched next to the offside back wheel. Taking the nail scissors, she stabbed the tyre as hard as she could. She rose quickly and walked on between the cars so she could come upon the building from a different direction. Having removed her cap, she entered the reception area and spoke to the administrator.

'Hello. I was driving past and noticed that one of the cars out the front has a flat tyre. I thought I'd let you know in case the owner hasn't spotted it,' she said in a concerned voice.

'Oh, that's kind of you,' the receptionist replied, smiling.

'It's no problem,' Sarah smiled back. 'I know what it's like when you're in a rush and you get to your car to find you can't go anywhere in a hurry.'

'You didn't happen to note the registration, did you? Or perhaps the make of the car?'

'I noticed the car as it's a rather nice Jaguar XJ. Here, I scribbled down the registration.' Sarah handed the slim, blonde woman a scrap of paper and waited whilst she looked in her records.

'Not one of our staff,' she murmured. 'Must be a visitor.'

Sarah watched as the receptionist ran a long slender finger, tipped with purple nail varnish, down the list of visitors' names.

'Ah, here it is; one of our regulars.' The woman picked up her phone.

Sarah tried to read the name upside down but couldn't quite make it out.

'Hi Harry, it's Theresa here. Please tell Mr Dubois that one of his tyres is flat.' She smiled at Sarah as she replaced the handset. 'That's your good deed done for the day. Thanks again.'

As Sarah turned to leave the phone rang again. While the receptionist was busy writing notes, she stole another quick look at the visitor sheet. The name written next to Dubois began with 'Xa'. She exited the building quickly and ran back to her car in case the man appeared.

Inside, Sarah brought up the Internet on her mobile and typed in *'putain'*. She discovered it was a slang French word with several meanings, most vulgar, depending on how it was used. One translation of the word was 'whore' and a related expression, *'fils de pute'*, translated as son of a bitch. That seemed to tie in with the fact that the man had spoken the word in an angry manner.

Next, she searched for French male names beginning with 'Xa'. 'Xander' and 'Xavier' were the top two. Sarah opened LinkedIn and entered 'Xander Dubois' but couldn't find anyone who looked like the man she sought. Then she ran a search for 'Xavier Dubois'. Well over a hundred results appeared. She examined the photos and found a match. He worked for Équipé Pharmaceuticals and his job title was given as "Directeur du Marketing". Sarah had never heard of the company. She scanned their website. They were located in France, in Rouen and Cahors.

She crossed her arms on the steering wheel and rested her chin on her hands, staring at the black Jaguar with its flat tyre. Though it might explain why he was here, knowing the stranger's name and occupation hadn't afforded her any clues regarding the past. Xavier; why did his name seem familiar? Then she realised the woman who had called her Suzette had also mentioned Xavier. She tried to recall exactly what had been spoken but couldn't. Hearing the word Suzette had been such a shock she hadn't thought about what else the stranger had said. Sarah sensed there had to be a connection between Suzette and this man and her memory was trying to reveal it.

She looked at her watch. It was nearly four o'clock. The pleasant afternoon sun, filtered by a large beech tree next to the road, was creating a dappled pattern on the bonnet of her Prius. No one had yet appeared to look at the Jag. It would be nearly five o'clock in France. She was determined to find out more.

Her French wasn't up to much, however, some of the Équipé Pharmaceuticals website was in English and Sarah figured it was therefore likely that the first point of contact for the company would be able to converse in English. She took a deep breath and dialled the Cahors number.

'Bonjour. Équipé Pharmaceuticals. Comment puis-je vous aider?' The woman spoke quickly.

Sarah spoke hesitantly, 'Ah, bonjour, Madame. Vous parlez anglais?'

'Oui. How can I 'elp you madame?' The voice was matter-of-fact and professional.

Sarah imagined an elegant, stylishly dressed lady. She summoned up her courage. 'Could I please speak to Monsieur Xavier Dubois?'

There was a pause. 'M. Dubois is out of the office at the

moment. Would you like to speak with someone else?'

Sarah felt her pulse increase. She'd picked the correct location. 'It's M. Dubois that I wanted to talk with. I'm ringing from the UK and was hoping to make contact to arrange a meeting for next time M. Dubois is in England. Do you know if he will be over here any time soon?'

'Wait a moment please. I'll connect you with 'is assistant.' The voice disappeared abruptly and Sarah's courage almost vanished with it. Shortly the silence was replaced by a deeper tone.

'Bonjour, madame. I am Louis Begnaud, assistant to M. Dubois. You wish for a meeting with 'im?'

Louis Begnaud sounded helpful, so Sarah decided to continue. 'Hello, M. Begnaud. Yes, I'm hoping to be able to meet with M. Dubois next time he's in the UK.'

'Can you tell me your name and company please?'

A rush of panic swept through Sarah's body and her stomach gave a lurch. 'Ah, yes, it's, er, Tina Saunders from, er...' she looked around frantically for inspiration, 'from Beech Chemicals,' she lied, hoping such a business did not exist. 'We're a start-up company. M. Dubois won't have heard of us,' she added hastily. 'Our IT people are working on a website at the moment.'

'I understand,' replied the assistant. 'Actually, you might be in luck, as M. Dubois 'appens to be in the UK at the moment. Mm, but wait a minute, 'e has a pretty full schedule I believe.'

'How long is he in the UK for?' Sarah ventured.

'I'm looking at 'is diary. Ah, 'e returns in nine days. Where is your company, Madame? 'E 'as meetings in many places,' the man rejoined then hesitated. 'Actually, it might be best if I ask 'im to call you.'

Sarah stalled. '*Merci*, M. Begnaud, you've been very helpful. If you could give me his mobile number, I'll call him and leave a message. Perhaps he might be able to fit in a brief meeting.' She took a further chance. 'Do you know which airport he'll be travelling back to France from? Maybe there'll be time for a quick chat there.'

'Per'aps,' Louis answered. Sarah could sense a shrug at the other end of the line. He read out the number. 'It's best if you speak with 'im. 'E flies from Birmingham. *Bonne après-midi, au revoir.*'

'*Au revoir, merci.*'

As Sarah put her phone away, she spotted a tall man in a dark blue suit walking out of the pharmaceutical company building and her stomach turned over again. It was Xavier Dubois. A few moments later a silver-grey Audi pulled into the car park and stopped in front of the Jaguar. A short red-haired man emerged, shook Dubois' hand and bent to look at the damaged tyre. He stood up again quickly and shrugged at Dubois. The two men proceeded to swap car keys and shook hands again. Sarah guessed Dubois had been given a replacement hire car. As the man from the hire company began to change the flat tyre for the emergency spare, Dubois got into the Audi and pulled out of the car park. Sarah was compelled to follow.

Chapter Ten

Dubois drove back into Great Malvern and continued south towards Malvern Wells, Sarah managing to stay a couple of cars behind. As the road cut into the incline, tracing the topography, he followed it, past numerous large old houses embedded in the broadleaf woodland which enveloped the steep rise of the hills. At length he turned right and followed a narrow lane rising further still, winding between tall hedges, past hidden dwellings and finally through the woodland. Sarah guessed Dubois was heading for the hotel that nestled amongst the trees about halfway from the summit. She hung back, ensuring that he was always couple of bends in the road ahead of her so that he wouldn't see her car in his mirrors.

Sarah swung into a segment of the car park away from where the Audi was parked. The hotel's parking area was carved into the hillside and prettily surrounded by shrubs and numerous species of conifer and flowering tree. Several large pink and white magnolias rose gracefully above an old Victorian gas lamp and a number of white Georgian buildings nestled amongst the verdant greenery. She continued to tail Dubois as he walked into the main entrance, passing a grassy terrace with a magnificent view over the Severn Vale towards the Cotswolds. It was warm and several people were indulging in alfresco afternoon tea. Strawberries and clotted cream and all manner of cakes and dainty sandwiches adorned tiered silver stands. Sarah looked at her watch. It was four-thirty. The scones and jam looked delicious, but she was still full of nervous tension and sensibly decided that the terrace offered little cover.

She entered the lounge bar via a small entrance hall paved with black and white diamond-shaped tiles. Dubois was making for a graceful, curved staircase up to the first floor. Sarah ordered a coffee and secreted herself in a corner of the lounge behind a newspaper. She considered what she hoped to gain by being there: perhaps she would overhear Dubois saying something that would trigger a different memory; maybe she could find out something more about him; she wanted him to lead her back to the woman who seemed to know Suzette. There must be a connection with both of them. Try as she might she still couldn't recall exactly what the woman had said. Did he know her twin? If she let him notice her, would he also mistake her for Suzette? Reflecting on this last thought, a multitude of consequences sped through her mind, the major one being that if Dubois did know her sister, given he'd had lunch with the woman who'd made a mistake and seemed keen to deny it, it was likely she would have told him. Sarah felt she shouldn't ignore the fear he'd sparked within her. He could be dangerous and having seen her who knows what might happen.

At five-twenty Dubois appeared in the bar having changed his suit in favour of a smart casual look. He ordered a beer and a glass of red wine and sat in one of two upright leather armchairs positioned in an alcove near a window, placing the drinks on a small round table between the chairs. Sarah threw a few furtive glances in his direction as she turned the pages and refolded her broadsheet. Within minutes his phone buzzed and he rose and walked out, leaving the drinks and his jacket.

Sarah walked to a window overlooking the car park with the pretence of studying an old black-and-white photograph on the wall. She could see Dubois greeting an elegant woman who had emerged from a dark green Mercedes. The anxiety gremlins in Sarah's abdomen lurched in unison and beads of perspiration began to prickle the skin on her forehead: it was the same woman she'd encountered earlier. The woman smoothed her navy pencil skirt and they kissed politely on both cheeks before walking in the direction of the building. Sarah scuttled back to her seat and resumed her position half-hidden behind the newspaper as they entered the bar. The woman looked to be in her late fifties. Her wide dark eyes and generous mouth, beautifully accentuated with deep red lipstick, perfected her dusky complexion. She wore her hair in a neat French pleat and her wraparound blouse complemented her skirt, showing off her trim figure.

While enjoying their drinks Dubois and the woman talked in earnest. Sarah noted that they didn't touch, although they frequently smiled at one another. After a while Dubois rose and walked in the direction of the staircase. Thirty seconds later she followed.

Sarah was again unsure what she should do. She reasoned that she could simply be a friend or colleague; however, there was something about their behaviour that spoke to her of an illicit liaison. Sarah inferred they were having an affair from the smiles they exchanged—their expressions exceedingly affectionate for business colleagues—coupled with the guarded nature of their physical contact.

Sarah bought a packet of crisps from the bar and settled down again, texting Ben to say that she was likely to be late home. Within a few minutes he replied, telling her not to worry and reminding her that he had a couple of clients that evening anyway. Sarah smiled to herself as she thought lovingly of Ben. He was always so supportive. He never put pressure on her or complained when she worked late or an urgent project hijacked their weekend. Each understood and respected the other's enjoyment of their chosen occupation and their desire to do well. Since they both had busy schedules, they greatly valued their time together and liked to ramble the heaths and woodland of the Malvern Hills, appreciating the changes each new season afforded. She glanced out of the nearest window. An acer bathed in the evening sun glowed fierily and the petals of the magnolias were blushed a rosy pink. Ben would love it here, she thought. But what would he think of her activities today? She wondered if he'd disapprove of her vandalism of Dubois' car; she would have thought it rash herself if there hadn't been a reason for it.

She finished her crisps and looked at her watch; it was nearly seven. The couple appeared in the bar ten minutes later. The woman had something of a glow; she'd changed into a low-cut, figure-hugging green cocktail dress. They ordered more drinks and headed for the restaurant.

Sarah didn't see any point in staying there. It was clear that they intended to spend the night at the hotel. She decided to go home, talk it over with Ben and return in the morning. On the way to her car she noted down the registration number of the woman's Mercedes.

Ben was still out when she arrived at their cottage, so she busied herself making him a quick meal of pesto pasta with chorizo and green beans. She guessed he would simply have had a sandwich earlier, as he'd missed their planned lunch. By the time he returned she'd opened a bottle of Malbec and his dinner was ready. She listened while he told her about his day and let him enjoy his meal before recounting her day.

'I've something to tell you and I'd like you to hear all of it before you ask me questions,' she began, topping up their glasses.

'God, that sounds ominous,' Ben responded lightly. His smile quickly turned to a frown as he saw the serious look on her face. Concerned, he laid a hand on her arm. 'Is everything okay? Are you alright?'

'Yes, I'm okay, but I need to talk about something that happened today.'

'Of course, sweetheart. Here, let me take your glass. Let's make ourselves more comfortable.'

They moved from the kitchen into their cosy lounge and settled themselves on the sofa. Outside, the daylight had dimmed to dusk and a gentle breeze played around the corners of the cottage, occasionally catching the slender new stems of a climbing rose and nudging them against the brickwork. The rose was in bud and would soon be framing the windows in pretty lemon. Sarah took a deep breath and told Ben everything that had happened, how she had felt and what she had done.

Apart from exclaiming 'Jesus, Sarah,' a couple of times, Ben kept his word and remained silent until Sarah had finished. His first reaction was excitement. 'Suzette's alive!

That's wonderful.' He was slightly taken aback at Sarah's uncharacteristic behaviour but admitted he would have punctured the tyre of a stranger's car in the same circumstances. However, the fact she had effectively stalked a strange man she believed might be dangerous filled him with apprehension. Nevertheless, he remarked that in the three years they'd been together he'd never known her to act injudiciously, so he knew there'd be a good reason for her actions.

They were sitting cross-legged facing one another on their two-seater couch. She'd been animated while talking but now remained quiet, her hands lying somewhat shakily in her lap. Ben took them in his and gave them a squeeze.

'Whatever's happened, I promise we'll get to the bottom of it and we will find her. You never remember your dreams, so it's weird you should experience such a strong image. And it's unlikely to be a dream as the bloke was sitting a few feet from you at the time. I agree, it does appear you've seen him before and, from the sound of it, not in a pleasant situation. The question is, when and where? Are you sure you didn't see him coming into the bistro before you had your funny turn? You couldn't have had a bit of *déjà vu* and that was somehow mixed up with hearing him?'

'I'm absolutely sure I didn't see him in the bistro,' Sarah responded resolutely. 'It was when I heard his voice that the image of his face came to me. I didn't actually see Dubois until he left the café.'

Ben ran a hand over his stubble, cupping his chin. 'Well, from what you've told me, there's obviously a link between Dubois, you having seen him before, this woman and Suzette. The fact that you visualised Dubois with a bundle in his arms and also Suzette's face speaks to me of a connection. Plus, the name Xavier is uncommon, so when that woman spoke to you she must have been referring to the same man she had lunch with.' He paused, tapping a finger against his lips in concentration. Then he spoke slowly, nodding his head slightly with each sentence as he followed his own logic. 'I'm trying to get my head around this. If you experienced a memory from when you were young, a bad memory that you'd locked away and forgotten about, and Dubois somehow triggered this memory to re-emerge, then it follows Dubois is in some way associated with the bad emotions. But as we don't know when this memory comes from—how old you were—we can't tell how emotionally mature you were at the time. So we can't know whether Dubois did something bad, something intentional which scared you, or whether you were frightened and anxious because you didn't understand what was going on.'

'Obviously I need to ask my parents about Dubois. They should know him, if him being near me was above board.'

'Yeah sure, but if he's connected with Suzette will they tell you the truth? I hate to say this, but if your mum and dad are complicit in some way, they could possibly warn Dubois off, although I admit that sounds dramatic.'

Sarah shrugged dejectedly. She'd noted sadly that the hard-won trust Ben had eventually placed in her parents had been eroded. 'Who knows? I need to hear their reaction to his name, at least. Dubois has something to do with this; I know he has,' she uttered. 'I can't get the horrible wailing out of my head and feeling so...

anguished; it was like having a nightmare in the middle of the day.' A single teardrop made its solitary way down her cheek and she abruptly swiped it with the back of her hand. She wasn't going to let this get the better of her. She took a large gulp of wine.

Ben patted her thigh and let his hand rest there. 'Okay, so if, and we have no proof that this is the case, if Dubois kidnapped your sister, we need to consider why he would do it. She's not dead, thank God, so we can rule that out.'

Sarah dismissed another possibility. 'Well, kids get kidnapped for ransoms but I can't see that being likely. Mum and Dad have never been wealthy and that was especially true when I was young. I suppose some children get taken because someone wants a child and can't have one.'

'So, maybe Dubois and the woman who thought you were Suzette wanted a child? The fact they went upstairs separately in the hotel might have implied an affair but perhaps this isn't the case, perhaps they're a couple.' A slight furrow appeared between Ben's eyebrows. 'That you were mistaken for your sister means Dubois' friend, wife, whoever she is, knows or has seen Suzette as an adult,' Ben continued methodically. 'So that suggests either they brought her up or they're in touch with her or the people who raised her.'

Sarah nodded. 'That makes sense. But why her? I mean, is there a connection? Or did they just see Mum and Dad with twins and thought "we'll have one of theirs?"' she offered disparagingly.

Ben shrugged. 'I suppose it's not beyond the realms of reason that a childless couple could think it unfair that others should have two babies when they have none.'

A wave of fear flushed through Sarah. 'Oh God, if he took her, what did he... do with her? I can't bear to think... I mean, someone who could kidnap a baby could be capable of anything.'

'Don't,' Ben interrupted. 'I know we're sitting here conceiving scenarios involving Dubois, but we don't know for definite he took Suzette. We can't even be certain your vision is real or, if it's, I don't know, the product of several, unrelated images, all thrown together. But if he did kidnap Suzette because he and the woman wanted a baby, they would surely have taken good care of her.'

Sarah reflected on his words, knowing he was trying to reassure her, and swallowed her trepidation, sending it back to her stomach. 'I follow your reasoning. All I can say is my gut tells me I saw Dubois do something that terrified me. I've tried to remember more. I can't recollect my parents in all of this, either. How old do you have to be to remember things as a child?'

'I don't know. We could ask Adam,' Ben suggested.

'I'm not sure whether childhood memory is within a neurologist's field,' replied Sarah. 'But if he doesn't know he'll probably know someone who does. Good thinking.'

'Can you try to recall more of what the woman said to you?' Ben suggested.

How had the woman come to say her sister's name? She'd been so preoccupied with the fact it was uttered, she couldn't recall the context. Ben kept silent, rising to pour them both another glass of red, emptying the bottle. Sarah sat quietly, focussing her mind. Eventually she was able to evoke the moments just before the woman had spoken. She had been looking at her phone, enjoying the warmth of the sun on her back then...

Had she said the word café? Maybe she'd mentioned something about a venue? Sarah grabbed her phone from the arm of the sofa, brought up a translate web page and typed 'venue'. It meant 'come' in French. That was it! The woman had asked her a question: did you come? Suddenly she could hear the stranger's voice, '*Es-tu venu avec Xavier?*'

The enormity of the phrase hit Sarah like a ton of bricks. 'Have you come with Xavier?'

Thirty minutes later Sarah had repeatedly phoned both her parents' mobile numbers, only to hear their voicemail messages. Frustrated, she'd left an exasperated message on her dad's phone insisting he call her back. She hadn't wanted to mention Dubois to avoid giving them prior warning. She needed to hear their gut reaction. She looked at her watch, yawned and stretched her legs out. 'I'm going to have to go to bed,' she declared. 'I'm wasted and I want to get to the hotel early tomorrow morning to catch Dubois leaving after breakfast.'

'What d'you mean? You're not going back there alone, are you?'

Sarah gave him an indomitable look.

'But what d'you hope to gain? You know his name and you said yourself you can't remember anything more,' Ben contended gently. 'And you mustn't be spotted.'

'Yes, but I'm hoping he might trigger another memory. And anyway, we need to find out more about her.'

Ben took a deep breath and ran one hand over his face, letting it come to rest cupping his mouth and chin while he considered Sarah's intentions. 'Look, you know I admire your determination and I couldn't stop you, even if

I wanted to, but I'm concerned for your safety if you track them alone. I can't come to the hotel with you, I'm supervising a couple of gym sessions, but I'll meet you mid-morning. Keep texting me to let me know where you are. Don't approach either of them, don't let them see you and stay where there are a lot of people, okay?'

Sarah nodded.

'Promise?' prompted Ben.

'I promise. I'll be careful, don't worry. I won't drive out of the Malvern area if it looks like they're heading somewhere else.' She held out her arms and he shifted toward her and gave her a big hug. 'Thank you,' she whispered into his ear.

He gave her a squeeze. 'What for?'

She pulled away slightly to look at him. 'For understanding. For being you,' she smiled.

That night Sarah dreamed that a man crept into her bedroom. Through the gloom she saw that he carried a bundle wrapped in cloth. Something in the bundle moved. The man's dark eyes bore into her. An abysmal howl began. He turned abruptly and left the room, but the wailing continued, on and on and...

Sarah woke in a sweat, feeling utterly bereft. She was now sure the wail had been coming from her.

Chapter Eleven

The following day was Saturday. The eager early morning sun thrust a bright beam through a gap in the heavy curtains screening Ben and Sarah's bedroom from the outside world, the shaft of light bisecting their bed, glimmering between the pillows. Dust motes stirred softly and slowly in the peaceful air. Sarah was lying on her back gazing at the tiny particles, enjoying the brief serenity afforded to her by concentrating on them.

She hadn't slept well following her dream. Ben had woken her after he'd been roused by her strangled moan. He'd enveloped her in his arms for a while as they lay, spooning, trying to get back to sleep. It was comforting and she'd forced herself to focus on the warmth of his body and the reassuring weight of the arm lying curved across her. A fitful sleep had eventually come.

They were up, showered, dressed and out of the house by seven-thirty. Sarah drove back to the hotel. The car park was fairly full however she found a space right at the far end near one of two whitewashed lodges. She was relieved to see the woman's Mercedes and Dubois' rented Audi. There was nothing to do but wait.

A few hotel guests came and went but otherwise there was little activity for an hour or so and Sarah attempted to relax by observing the wildlife through her windscreen.

The trees planted in the hotel grounds and the woodland on the slope of the hill behind were host to all kinds of birdlife. Industrious blackbirds and all manner of tits sought insects amongst the branches, chaffinches busied themselves in the undergrowth and a robin was occupied with a worm in one of the flower beds. She caught a flash of pink and blue as a jay flew out of the trees into a small group of conifers to her right, an acorn in its beak. The familiar cooing of wood pigeons joined the melodies of birdsong, which at any other time Sarah would have found soothing. Not today. She tried to identify the feelings stirring uneasily within. Trepidation, dread, an aching longing? A distillation of these, and more, with no name. She wanted to gather and extract the emotional amalgam and hold it to the light, as the squirming annelid in the beak of the robin.

Just then she caught sight of the couple emerging from the main building into the glorious sunshine. They were casually dressed and both wore running shoes. Sarah glanced at her watch; it was nine-thirty. The pair got into Dubois' car and proceeded out of the car park. Sarah quickly started her Toyota and followed them back into Great Malvern and the parking zone she and Dubois used the day before. She continued downhill and was lucky to find a space, as the area was busy with Saturday shoppers. She donned a baseball cap, walked back to the vicinity of the Audi and waited behind a group of trees while the couple put on walking boots, then followed as they went uphill, turning onto Bellevue Terrace where Sarah first saw Dubois.

After a short distance they crossed the Rosebank public gardens and climbed the so-called 'Ninety-nine

Steps' leading to a track that snaked up through the heavily wooded valley between North Hill and the Worcestershire Beacon. Sarah guessed they would head for St Ann's Well, an old spring well-known locally and featured in all the guidebooks. She took her time climbing the steep, narrow steps, principally because the passageway housing them curved around to the right towards the top and she didn't wish to come across Dubois suddenly if he stopped to rest or look at a map before reaching the path that eventually led to the summit of the Beacon. There would be no room to pass without being seen at close quarters.

Ascending, Sarah reminisced about childhood walks with her parents, who were always keen on outdoor pursuits. They had owned a shop selling outdoor gear and fishing tackle in Upton-on-Severn for thirty years. As a family they'd explored most of the hills, though St Ann's Well had been her favourite place; not least because the pretty hexagonal Victorian café there sold delicious ice cream and she loved drinking ice-cold water straight out of the hillside. She'd trodden this path countless times and, as a child, would always count each step. There weren't quite ninety-nine nowadays and perhaps never had been. She refrained from counting them now; she had to keep her wits about her.

As she followed the winding track, Sarah made sure to keep the peak of her cap low across her forehead and tried to keep her targets within distant sight. She'd texted Ben, asking him to meet her near the back of the café, nestled comfortingly into the hill about halfway to the summit. Once there, she positioned herself a little way up the slope from steps to a chamber above the café, from where she could see the main entrance without being obvious to anyone going in and out. Dubois and his friend had entered the engaging stone Well Room, where the spring supplied a gentle flow of Malvern water through a white marble dolphin's head into a basin elaborately carved to resemble a shell. After a while they emerged and took a walk around the gardens at the front of the building. Sarah watched and waited for Ben.

Ben located Sarah as the couple entered the teashop. Having jogged up the hill he was somewhat breathless and perspiring in the unusually warm mid-morning sunshine.

'I could do with a cold drink,' he panted as he sat on the grass, flexing his tired legs. 'Where are they? What's the plan?'

Sarah had been contemplating their next move for some time. 'Would you mind trying to strike up a conversation with them? Casual banter, to try to obtain some information. Perhaps you could engage in a bit of small talk in the café?'

Ben shot her a reluctant expression.

'Please, Ben. I'd do it but for obvious reasons I can't,' Sarah pleaded. 'You're good at small talk, you know, with clients, and there won't be any trouble, they don't know you from Adam.'

'Okay, I'll do it for you, Miss Lester,' he assented, rolling his eyes as he heaved himself to his feet.

As Ben made his way to the café entrance below, Dubois and the woman exited and climbed the steps on the opposite side, which curved up to meet a path leading around the back of the building and onto the hillside. He glanced back at Sarah who was heading towards the pump room to avoid being spotted. He popped into the café to buy an ice lolly before following the couple at a distance as they strolled through woodland and out onto a small outcrop, in the middle of which sat a small, circular metal seat with a curved back, whose green paint had been worn to grey in places by countless bottoms and the tiny shoes of children running on it excitedly.

When he caught up with the couple, they were sitting with their backs to him, admiring the view. He sat on the nearest part of the seat and gazed in the opposite direction, listening in on their conversation. They didn't say anything noteworthy, simply appreciating the landscape. He heard Dubois call the woman *"ma petite souci"* at one point; while his French wasn't up to much, he recognised the first two words and guessed that this could perhaps be a term of endearment.

He finished his lolly, rose and stretched, stepping a little nearer to the couple. 'Beautiful day, isn't it?' he ventured, looking at them. The woman's hair was piled up in an elegant yet casual way that complemented her fine sculptured features and showed off her long, graceful neck.

She gave him a smile. 'Yes, lovely and so warm.' She spoke with no discernible accent.

'Perfect for a hike,' Ben replied, smiling back. 'Are you walking far?'

'We don't know the area,' Dubois contributed, adjusting his position to look at Ben, 'we're just going to go to the top.'

'Ah, well, there's more than one summit around here,' Ben answered kindly. 'From here you can go that way,' he pointed, 'to the top of Sugarloaf Hill, or that way,' he indicated south, 'to the top of the Worcestershire Beacon. There are actually fifteen hills in this range; the Beacon is the highest.'

The couple looked at one another for a moment and the woman inclined her head slightly in a silent question. Dubois shrugged. 'I don't mind. It's a nice day and we 'ave plenty of time.'

'There's a gorgeous patch of bluebells in the woodland over there and plenty of paths, so it's not difficult to do a circular walk wherever you are,' Ben said helpfully. 'I'm Ben, by the way.'

'Xavier,' nodded Dubois.

The woman hesitated for a moment. 'Elizabeth,' she responded, avoiding Dubois' dark eyes. Momentarily there appeared a slight twitch at the corner of Dubois' mouth.

'Are you on holiday?' Ben tried to keep his tone light.

The woman opened her mouth to reply but let Dubois answer. 'Visiting for the weekend,' came his heavily accented retort. His next words were spoken to her. 'Come, Elizabeth, let's continue our walk.'

'I came for the weekend a few years ago and sort of never left. I love it here,' Ben said, hoping to find out a bit more. 'Have you come far?'

'France.'

'Devon.'

They responded simultaneously, not looking at Ben as they gathered their things and stood.

'Ah. My girlfriend went to college in Devon. Exeter actually. Do you know Exeter?' Ben lied cheerfully.

'Thank you for the information,' Dubois said politely, as he turned to go, indicating the conversation was over.

'It was nice to meet you,' Elizabeth added.

Ben watched them walk back along the outcrop then turn south, towards the top of the Beacon. He reflected on what he had learned. It didn't seem much.

'Her name is Elizabeth and she lives in Devon, so not with him, it seems, if he's in France. They act affectionately with one another and he called her his little *sousi*,' he recounted to Sarah as they made their way back down the hill towards the town. 'That's all. He was polite but fairly non-committal. She seemed nice. I noticed that she was wearing a wedding ring and he wasn't.'

'Are you sure it was *sousi*, s.o.u.s.i?' Sarah asked, tapping on her phone. 'Nothing's coming up in Translate. *Sourir* means smile. Perhaps he said "my little smile"? No, that doesn't sound right. Or it might have been *souris*, that means mouse. "My little mouse" could be an affectionate term.'

'No, I'm sure it was *sousi*; it sounded like that anyway.' Ben frowned as he tried to recall Dubois' accent.

'How about *souci* with a c? S.o.u.c.i. The c is pronounced as an s. *Souci* is a type of flower or it can mean worry, anxiety, problem or trouble. That might fit, "my little problem", if they're having an affair.'

'She did seem hesitant before she gave me her name,' he offered. 'Perhaps she was being cautious, though he gave me his real name.'

Sarah turned to him and grabbed both his hands. 'Thank you,' she said earnestly. 'I appreciate your support; it means a lot to me.'

Ben smiled and squeezed her hands. Then he gave her a big hug. 'I love you, sweetheart. I'll always support you.'

'Even when I'm a batty old woman?' she laughed.

'Especially when you're a batty old woman. You're halfway there already.'

'Hey, less of the old if you don't mind,' she grinned. 'Actually, all this investigating is exciting, isn't it? I'm almost beginning to enjoy it.'

'Hmm. I'm not so sure.' He couldn't hold onto his smile. 'We don't know who we're dealing with, remember? This man is giving you nightmares. Come on, let's go and have a drink and some lunch.'

As they walked the remainder of the path into Malvern, hand in hand, Ben mulled over the situation. Sarah's positivity and excitement were typical of her, as was her obvious stimulation by a mystery to solve. She had a reasoning, scientific mind and loved a challenge. However, he'd never seen her so negatively affected by anyone. As if she'd been thrown off balance. He also knew that she wouldn't stop until she'd got to the bottom of it and was liable to neglect her own safety to achieve her purpose: that worried him.

Chapter Twelve

Later that day Sarah made three phone calls. The first was to Jennifer.

'Hi Jen. Hope all's well in the Gray household. Look, there's been a development. But before I go into that, could you please ask Adam what age a child is when they begin to remember things, in general I mean?'

'Yes, sure. I guess you want to know whether it's possible you could recall something about your twin?' Jennifer speculated.

'Yes, in a manner of speaking.'

After speaking with Jennifer, Sarah phoned Andy Finch and asked if he would search for newspaper reports of kidnap, in case his previous search for a missing person report hadn't covered all angles. She confided in him about Xavier Dubois, Elizabeth and her visions. She knew Andy had an open mind; he'd certainly proved that in the past.

He listened patiently then spoke decisively. 'Sarah, if you're saying you believe you recall seeing this man in your room when you were a toddler and that he had something in his arms you think may have been your sister, I believe you. It's not like you to chase a fantasy. You have an analytical, logical mind and I've never known you to take anything but a reasoned approach. In fact, that's precisely what you're doing now, isn't it? Investigating one option after another, ruling out some scenarios and including others, working towards the truth.'

Sarah felt bolstered by his analysis of her. Andy said he'd run a new search the following day and get in touch.

Sarah waited until the early evening before calling her father. She wanted to catch her parents before they set off for the day. To her relief Jake answered, his warm and welcoming tenor arousing hope. Maybe she could get something more from him today.

'Hello, love. Sorry we 'an't been in touch for a while. This holiday's like a whirlwind. Everythin's okay though. Sorry if we've worried you. We would've contacted you if there'd been a problem. So don't fret, love, okay? Anyway, how are you? Oh, hang on, yer mum wants a word.'

Sarah could barely control her patience while Lena, hardly drawing breath, excitedly recounted the places that they'd visited over the past couple of weeks. Her folks were clearly having the holiday of a lifetime, but their obvious joy cast a greater shadow over their undoubted deception. Finally, her mum asked how she was and what she'd been doing.

Sarah requested the phone be switched to speaker mode and took a deep breath. 'A woman in the street mistook me for someone else. She called me Suzette. When I questioned her, she said she was mistaken.' Sarah tried to keep exasperation from tainting her tone. 'Then in a bistro I heard a man's voice talking in French and had the most horrid experience. A distinct vision of this man's face came into my head and I felt dreadful; afraid and despairing. And then…'

'Oh love, that sounds awful. You sound like you had a funny turn,' Jake interjected sympathetically. 'I have those sometimes,' he continued quickly. 'Must run in the family.'

'This wasn't a funny turn, Dad,' Sarah stated emphatically. 'I saw the man coming out of the café and he looked exactly like my vision, except older. It was like I was remembering something from when I was young and I have a horrible feeling about him. I heard him called Xavier. You must know him.'

There was a pause then Jake spoke again and Sarah detected a distinct shake in his voice. 'I recall a Xavier who came to a barbeque at our house one time when you were a toddler. He was a friend of a friend I think. I remember him shoutin' a lot, 'cause he got very drunk. So maybe he scared you. Well, fancy you should remember that. It must have made a lastin' impression. But there's no cause t' be concerned love.'

'He was with the woman who'd called me Suzette,' she continued determinedly. 'That's a hell of a coincidence, mistaking me for someone with the name of my twin.'

Another pause. Sarah noted that her mum had become unusually quiet. 'I don't rightly know what yer sayin', love,' Jake replied, his tone firm and even, 'but a coincidence is all it is. Yer sister's dead, so it can't be anythin' else. The woman said she'd made a mistake is all. Listen, you sound like you could do with a break. Get away fer a bit and recharge yer batteries; you'll feel better for it.'

'But Dad…'

'We've gotta go now,' Jake spoke hurriedly, 'we've a boat t' catch. We'll be in touch in a few days. Don't worry yerself an' give our love to that man of yours. Bye, love.'

The phone went dead.

Sarah told Ben Jake's fabricated story about Xavier Dubois. Over dinner that evening they discussed what they knew so far and how they might proceed.

Dubois clearly knew Suzette and since Elizabeth also knew her, then she might be in England or France. Were Dubois and Elizabeth a couple? They could be now at least, if not in the past. Some relationships were conducted over long distances; some men didn't wear wedding rings; perhaps they simply weren't married. If they had raised Suzette, what surname would she have? Elizabeth's last name was unknown, but they had 'Dubois' as a starting point. They searched for 'Suzette Dubois' in Google, on Facebook and LinkedIn. They found no one with that name who looked like Sarah.

So, if not Dubois, what next? She could have one of millions of names. She might be married herself. They decided the next step must be to obtain more information from Elizabeth, if she could be persuaded to part with it, and, in order to track her, they somehow had to discover her surname and address.

Sarah asked Ben to contact a friend of his who worked at the Driver and Vehicle Licensing Agency in Swansea, to see whether he could be persuaded to investigate the address matching the car Elizabeth drove. Ben pointed out that the details of a vehicle owner's address were private and his friend Matt could get into trouble if he gave out confidential details; he would probably lose his job if he were found out. Sarah visited the DVLA website, finding that only general information on the number of previous owners was available, although she noted wryly that parking charge firms could buy current keeper information, albeit through a tightly regulated process.

However, she discovered that a request for details of a car's registered keeper could be made if there was reasonable cause, although this was supposed to be logged using a specified form. Whilst acknowledging they would be attempting to obtain personal information unlawfully, she swayed Ben to speak to his friend.

They agreed Ben would say he wanted to find out who'd been responsible for accidentally knocking him off his bike, as the driver hadn't noticed and drove off; however, he didn't want to involve the police or register his details, he simply wanted to write to the motorist telling them to be more cyclist-aware. Ben was adamant they should not log a false inquiry with the DVLA in writing, as that would mean providing their details and he wanted no trace of a connection to the woman. He would ask Matt for a favour and hope his friend would bend the rules.

As they were curled up in bed that night, Sarah's mind kept replaying the moment the stranger had called her Suzette.

'Ben, are you still awake?' she whispered as she rolled over to face him.

'Mmm,' came his drowsy reply.

'I've been thinking how lucky I was to encounter that woman who mistook me for Suzette and fortunate I'd learned about my sister before I bumped into her. Otherwise the name Suzette wouldn't have meant anything to me and I wouldn't have discovered Dubois. I think it was fate.'

Ben opened his eyes and smiled tenderly. 'You sound like Jen,' he replied sleepily.

She returned his affectionate look. 'It's not surprising,' she acknowledged, 'knowing what happened to her. She wouldn't have met Adam if she hadn't been in that coma. There's a part of me now that's sure fate alters people's lives,' she shrugged, 'while another voice is telling me it's just coincidence.'

Ben drew her to him so she was snuggled into his shoulder. His body was warm and comforting.

'From what you've told me, Dubois is a regular visitor to that company in Malvern, so it's feasible you could have encountered him before, or might have done at some point in the future,' he replied sagely. 'You probably just happened to be in the same place at the same time.'

'I suppose so,' Sarah agreed. 'I guess people view coincidence differently: pure chance or accident, or else serendipity, fate, destiny even.' She sighed wearily then yawned. 'Anyway, whatever it is I have a feeling it was meant to be.'

That Monday morning at work Sarah couldn't concentrate. She tried processing data, but her mind kept wandering. She checked emails, answered minor enquiries and wrote marketing correspondence. Several mugs of coffee later she went outside to get some air. The day was fresh and breezy. Fluffy cumulus clouds scurried across a light grey sky and the pink and red poppies growing around the perimeter of the building nodded happily. She rang Ben for an update. To her surprise and relief he had news.

'Got it,' Ben stated, sounding self-satisfied.

'Really?' Sarah was eager to receive a positive result after the blanks they'd recently drawn.

'Yep, Matt gave me an address. Purely off the record. You can't ever tell anyone where it came from, okay?'

'Yes, of course. Where does she live?' Sarah was impatient.

'Well, the car is registered, not to an Elizabeth, but a Marigold Thomas. She lives in Newton Ferrers, in Devon.'

'That's odd. Why would she say she was Elizabeth?'

'There could be several reasons,' Ben replied objectively. 'Perhaps the car belongs to this Marigold Thomas and the Elizabeth woman borrowed it or she's having an affair with Dubois and wants to protect her identity, so gave a fake name or, I don't know, it's her middle name and she prefers using it. Even if the car belongs to someone else it's reasonable to suppose that it's a friend of hers who probably lives in the vicinity. So we know where she lives.'

'Unless she's stolen it,' Sarah suggested. Suspicion of Dubois and anyone he was associated with had lodged in her mind.

'If she'd stolen it the DVLA would probably have a record of that and Matt would have told me,' corrected Ben patiently. 'Where's your logical head today, sweetheart?'

'Okay, yeah, so where does that get us? We know she's associated with Dubois and probably lives in Devon, although we don't know whether she is Marigold Thomas.' Sarah ran a hand through her hair, tapping her head with two fingers, contemplating.

'*Souci*!' remarked Ben triumphantly.

'What?'

'Dubois called the woman "*ma petite souci*", remember? We looked the phrase up and, if we had the spelling right,

111

it seemed to mean worry or trouble, or it's a type of flower. I've just looked up the word again: it can mean Marigold! How about that?' For a moment Ben's enthusiasm bubbled over into elation. 'Hey, I've actually solved something.'

'Ben, that's brilliant.' Sarah was thrilled. 'So she is Marigold Thomas and lives in Newton Ferrers and we have the exact address. Now we can find out more about her and whether she's had any dodgy dealings with Dubois,' Sarah stated excitedly.

'Hmm,' was Ben's cautious response. 'We'll have to tread carefully if we're going to try to obtain information from her. I'm not sure how much closer this gets us to finding out why Dubois might have kidnapped your sister, or to finding her.'

'Ben, it's a huge step forward. This woman, Marigold, knows Suzette and associates her with Dubois. One of them can lead us to my sister, I know they can. Any link to Dubois may be a potential source of information about him and any information could be useful.' Sarah directed her surge of positivity to lift Ben on its swell. This was often the case.

'Yeah, I guess so.'

'I'll see you at home, okay?'

'Okay, see you later, sweetheart.'

'Ben?'

'Yes?'

'Love you.'

'Love you too.'

Ten minutes after arriving home that evening Sarah's phone pinged, announcing the arrival of a text. 'It's from

Jen,' she said, swiping the screen. 'Adam has answered our question about early childhood memory.'

'What does he say?' Ben asked.

Sarah fell quiet.

'Come on, spill the beans,' Ben urged.

Sarah took a deep breath. 'He says that although adults are usually only able to remember events from about the age of three, due to something called childhood amnesia, research has shown children can remember memories from earlier ages and that infants' bodies can chemically reflect trauma. Adam said that in young children who don't have the ability to describe a trauma, it's still stored in their brains and can disrupt aspects of their childhood development. They may not remember specific events, but they do remember emotions and images. He goes on to say that as we get older our earliest memories decline but he couldn't rule out the recollection of a traumatic image.'

Sarah looked at Ben decisively. 'The image of Dubois is real. He was in my bedroom, he took my sister and I saw the whole thing.'

Chapter Thirteen

Plymouth, England, 30 May 2018

Sarah and Jennifer had turned south off the Devon Expressway and were nearing the village of Newton Ferrers. Sarah had discussed the situation with Jennifer and asked if she could accompany her to Devon for a couple of days, suggesting they meet in Bristol, four hours by train from York, and the next morning she'd drive them from there. Ben had been unable to change his shifts for the remainder of that week but had booked the following ten days off work. He was uneasy about the idea of Sarah and Jennifer pursuing Marigold Thomas. However, he thought it infinitely better than Sarah continuing the investigation alone, which she was otherwise resolved to do. As luck had it, Adam's hospital rota enabled him to look after Emily for a couple of days, allowing Jennifer to help her friend. Jennifer said this good fortune was fated and was sure that, together, they'd be able to uncover key information.

Sarah was relieved and grateful to have Jennifer with her. Although nervous, she was determined to discover more about Dubois. Though dogged in her pursuit of the truth, she felt safer having an ally by her side; someone with whom to discuss strategy and a witness to whatever might happen. According to Jen, Adam had voiced reservations but hadn't tried to talk his wife out of the trip, however he counselled her to take care of herself and act judiciously. Sarah recognised that although there were still times when Jennifer's innate vulnerability surfaced, her susceptibility had diminished significantly in the time she and Adam had been together. However, as she'd rarely been apart from Emily for more than a couple of hours in the year since their daughter was born, Sarah realised that supporting her in her quest must be tremendously important to Jennifer.

The narrow road was bounded by high hedges, which soon gave way to low houses on either side. They passed a sign for a primary school and continued towards the centre of the village via a mixture of old whitewashed cottages, newer bungalows and the occasional small business. There was an abundance of greenery, from neat lawns to burgeoning shrubs and tall trees. Ivy proliferated on stone walls and delicate white wood sorrel grew in shady spots. Bluebells abounded and the pretty pink petals of red campion could be seen in the hedgerows. Led by her satnav, Sarah took a narrow lane down the hill which had a signpost for the harbour. They reached the creek, from where they could see the village of Noss Mayo gathered around an inlet on the other side of the blue-green water. A small stone cross stood in the middle of the tiny junction and on their left was an old inn overlooking the estuary.

'Do you remember that pub?' grinned Jennifer.

'It's more a case of what I don't remember,' Sarah laughed. 'Oh God, that weekend here during the Easter holidays; the second year we were at college.'

'We generated a lot of empty pint glasses. God knows how we got back up the hill.' Sarah's brow furrowed momentarily. 'Did we get into a rowing boat at some point?'

'Oh yeah... I think you're right.'

Sarah spotted a car coming down the hill behind them in her mirror. 'Oops, I'd better move; we're blocking the road here. Which way's the satnav pointing?'

'It wants you to go right,' Jennifer replied, 'down that narrow street.'

Sarah put the Prius in gear again and swung into a lane parallel to the water. It led to an expanded area of road by the edge of the creek, on one side of which was a slipway and several small boats. There was a handful of parking spaces, most empty as it was mid-morning. Jennifer suggested they leave the car there as she didn't think there would be room to park anywhere further up the lane.

They walked along the road past several painted terraced houses whose gardens ran down to the water. The way narrowed and rose slightly, leaving the surface of the little estuary further below them. Across the river the houses of Noss Mayo had petered out to be replaced by lush woodland whose trees blanketed the hillside and stretched out over the water's edge. The sun was breaking through thin clouds, the water turning a pretty green, reflecting the overhanging vegetation. Numerous small sailing boats bobbed gently on their moorings. Sarah had transferred the postcode of their destination to her phone and tracked their location. At length the app indicated they had arrived.

The dwellings on the hill above were mostly screened by tall hedges. There were no numbers displayed. They looked around for the name of the house they sought and found an attractive stone building with a slate roof charmingly situated right on the edge of the creek. The small parking area beyond a set of low wrought iron gates was empty, as they had hoped it would be. To be sure of Marigold's absence Jennifer knocked at the front door before scurrying to hide with Sarah down the road. No one answered. A couple of cars were parked in front of a modern-looking house opposite.

'That looks like a good bet,' remarked Sarah.

They had agreed Jennifer would do the talking so that if the neighbour subsequently gave Marigold a description it would be of her rather than Sarah. They approached the house and rang the doorbell.

The door was opened by a well-dressed woman in her mid-sixties, grey hair cut in a neat bob. She wore several expensive-looking rings and a substantial gold necklace. Jennifer apologised for disturbing her and explained that Marigold Thomas had been a school friend of her mother's and they wanted to talk to her about attending a surprise birthday party for her mum. Jennifer clarified that she didn't know Marigold but was trying to contact a number of former school friends. She asked the neighbour if she knew where Marigold worked. The lady, a Mrs Withers, helpfully informed them that Mari, as she called her, worked part-time these days, often from home, although she still visited the office in Plymouth. After a further minute or two the girls were in possession of the office address and the fact Marigold was a translator.

'Is there a Mr Thomas?' Jennifer asked politely. 'I'd like to invite him as well.'

'Oh, that could be a bit tricky,' the woman replied. 'You

see, they're getting a divorce. I think it best not to mention him. He's moved out now, but it's all been rather difficult.' She nodded sympathetically.

Jennifer thanked the woman, remarking that she had a lovely view.

'Yes, it's rather wonderful. The view from Mari's is even better. That's why she's fighting to keep the house,' she divulged indiscreetly.

'Well, that was a success,' Jennifer pronounced as they made their way back to the car.

Sarah nodded. 'Now the hard bit; how we approach her.'

'We'll stick to our guns; at least it will be in a public place.'

They drove the ten miles into Plymouth, discussing their next options. The office they sought was located within a smart street of three-storey houses behind the Hoe. Parking was kerbside and they had to drive a way down the road before they found a space. Sarah spotted the number plate of Marigold's car. She checked her watch; it was nearly noon.

They waited in the car for ten minutes or so then spotted their target exiting the office. She walked to her car and drove towards the city centre. They followed at a distance, Jennifer enthusiastically confirming directions. Eventually they found themselves on the eastern side of Sutton Harbour, where there were a number of modernised wharfs, contemporary apartments and office blocks. Marigold had pulled into a parking area adjacent to an old stone warehouse which was now an inn. A large stone-paved area to the nearside of the building, populated with wooden tables, was bustling with folk enjoying lunch; a narrower wooden deck running along the sides and front of the inn next to the water was also busy. Wooden steps led from the deck to the first floor. Sarah and Jennifer watched from a distance as Marigold checked the outside seating areas before entering. They waited a few moments before going in.

Inside, limestone walls reflected the sunshine pouring in through copious windows. In one section of the hostelry dark wooden A-frames supporting the roof two storeys above were splendidly exposed. An oak mezzanine floor, a remnant of the building's origins, was supported by wooden pillars. In many areas the roof was visible from the ground floor, adding to the air of spaciousness. The floor was mainly carpeted red, which lent a touch of opulence. On both floors the rooms were filled with tables set for lunch and lit by red table lamps. The place was filling up; the buzz of conversation and sound of laughter echoed off the walls.

Jennifer looked around for Marigold while Sarah bought a couple of drinks from the bar. Jennifer quickly reappeared.

'I've found them. She's actually with Dubois! I spotted a table not far from them where we can sit without being seen.'

At that moment a tall, clean-shaven man with light brown hair and hazel eyes arrived and shook hands warmly with one of the barmen. He spoke with a French accent and they seemed to know one another well. The barman called him Pierre and pointed to where Marigold and Dubois were sitting. The girls watched as Pierre joined his friends, before secreting themselves at a nearby table behind a wooden partition. They hoped to learn something of their targets' conversation, however, the ambient noise in the room was too loud to hear clearly, although they discerned a mixture of French and English. As they didn't know how long Dubois and his friends would stay and wanted to be able to leave at a moment's notice, Jennifer and Sarah merely ordered starters; scallops and calamari with garlic bread. The food was delicious.

It was clear the relationship between the three was warm and close. Dubois and Marigold had greeted Pierre with kisses and hugs. From time to time, Jennifer moved her chair to get a brief view of them. Marigold was behaving in the same friendly manner with both men, showing no signs of particular intimacy with Dubois. He was clearly not her husband, unless theirs was a remarkably amicable divorce which didn't fit what Mrs Withers had divulged. But her behaviour with Dubois in this public place, affectionate but not too intimate, did support Sarah's idea that she and Dubois were having an affair.

While having coffee, the girls paid for their meal and waited. They discussed the options for their next move; should they follow Marigold discreetly or confront her? At length they decided to shadow her until she was alone, then confront her. Although both girls recognised this could be a dangerous move, Jennifer had the advantage of anonymity.

At length the barman who was familiar with Pierre went to their table and Pierre settled the bill. He shook the barman's hand again and, patting him on the back, said something which made them all laugh.

'Look out, they're coming this way,' warned Jennifer.

Sarah ducked to retrieve her bag off the floor while Jennifer pretended to be interested in her coffee. The girls heard Marigold say she'd see the two men later. Pierre was looking at his watch. 'We'd better get to our meeting,' he told Dubois as they passed the girls' table.

Marigold went in the direction of the ladies' toilet and Dubois and Pierre departed for the car park. Jennifer followed the woman while Sarah walked to the bar and spoke to the man they'd seen talking with Pierre.

'Hi there. Lovely meal, thanks.'

'You're welcome,' he nodded, smiling.

'I think I saw an acquaintance head out of here. I don't know him well, but I'd like to say hello. The thing is, I've forgotten his name, which could be embarrassing. You seemed to know him—tall man with brown hair, French accent.'

'You mean Pierre?'

'Yes, that's him. Pierre... um ...what's his second name?'

'Marchand,' came the reply. 'Dr Marchand.'

'Oh, yes, I remember now,' lied Sarah. 'He works at... um was it the hospital? I thought so, but he might have moved.'

'You're warm,' chuckled the barman. 'It's the clinic near the hospital.' He looked towards the door. 'You'd better try and catch him, or he'll be gone.'

'Great, thanks so much.' Sarah ran to the door but once outside moved cautiously away, scanning the car park for Dubois. A red Maserati drove past barely ten feet away. She glimpsed Dubois in the passenger seat. Fortunately he was looking straight ahead. She made a note of the car's registration number although it was a recognizable vehicle. She sat at an empty table around the corner of the building out of sight of the main entrance and searched clinics in Plymouth on her phone, glancing up regularly for the appearance of Jennifer or Marigold.

In the meantime, Jennifer waited for Marigold to emerge from a cubicle then stood next to her, washing her hands. 'He's a nice guy, Monsieur Dubois.' She smiled to the woman.

'Excuse me?' replied Marigold, her brow furrowing.

'M. Dubois. I saw you having lunch with him. I was just saying what a nice man he is,' repeated Jennifer in a friendly manner.

Marigold shrugged slightly, shook her head and replied nonchalantly. 'Oh, is he? I hardly know him. He's a friend of a friend. I only met him today; he seemed pleasant.' She made to go, then turned back. 'How do you know him?'

'Business. I'm in pharmaceuticals,' answered Jennifer, trying to sound self-assured. The woman's dark eyes seemed to bore into her and Jennifer had the feeling that she was being scrutinised.

'Really,' she said flatly and walked out of the lady's room.

Jennifer took a deep breath. The woman was obviously hiding something. Why would she have lunch quite openly with the man then pretend not to know him? If she didn't want to be seen or associated with him they wouldn't have met in public. They clearly had something to conceal. Jennifer decided to use the loo before joining Sarah outside. She hoped her friend had managed to glean some new information.

Sarah spotted Marigold having emerged from the inn. Her back was towards Sarah and she was on her mobile clearly trying to make a call and failing to reach the recipient. As she walked through the car park, Sarah moved closer to listen, keeping her head down and crossing to the other side of a row of tall green shrubs separating the two rows of parking bays.

'Fuck,' Marigold swore and began to dial another number, stopping briefly to look back in the direction of the inn. Sarah noted that Jennifer had not yet appeared. Her heart was thumping so loud she felt as though Marigold would hear it. The woman appeared to be leaving a voicemail and Sarah strained to overhear.

'Hi, Fran, would you mind if we had dinner at yours this evening instead? I've had someone talk to me about Xavier, trying to find out how well I know him.' She spoke rapidly and Sarah discerned a rising anxiety in the timbre of her voice. 'It's got to be either Gerren's doing or something to do with that other wretched business. I didn't think Gerren would stoop so low as to hire a PI but if it is him, I can't risk him accusing me of an affair and losing the house. I'm not going to be blamed for deliberately wrecking a marriage which has long been broken. If it's linked with the other, and I bloody hope not, we'll all have to be careful. I can't get hold of Xavier right now. I'm beginning to think I shouldn't be phoning him at all. Would you be able to get a message to him through Pierre? Don't worry about cooking, I'll bring pizza.'

Marigold rang off and continued walking quickly towards her car. Sarah peered through a gap between the laurel and spotted the green Mercedes about fifteen feet away. She hesitated for a moment, unsure what to do.

"That other wretched business." Could that be her sister's kidnapping? "We'll all have to be careful." God, how many were involved? Who was Fran? What the hell was going on? Impelled by an overwhelming surge of anger, she pushed through the greenery and ran after her target, reaching her as she was opening her car door.

'Stop. I need to know where Suzette is. She's my twin, for God's sake! I know you know her. Tell me where she is,' cried Sarah, reaching out to put her hand on Marigold's arm.

Mari whipped around, shock widening her eyes and pulling at her mouth. 'Oh.'

Sarah glimpsed a fleeting shadow of something else crossing her features. Was it fear?

She shook Sarah's hand off her arm indignantly. 'What the… are you following me? I told you I made a mistake. I don't know your sister. Now excuse me, I have to go.'

Jennifer appeared, breathless, at Sarah's side. Marigold climbed into the car and tried to pull the door shut but Jennifer stepped forward to block it with her body.

'You again,' Mari looked at Jennifer with disdain. 'What do you think you're doing? Get away from my car,' she barked.

Sarah crouched to look Mari in the eyes more easily. She managed to produce a calm menacing tone. 'I don't believe you've made a mistake. I know Xavier Dubois is connected with my sister Suzette. You mentioned Xavier and Suzette. It's too much of a coincidence, don't you think?'

Mari fumbled with her car key, her hands visibly shaking. She managed to insert it into the ignition and kept her right hand on the key ring, presumably in case

Sarah or Jennifer should try to take it. She gripped the steering wheel with her other hand, fingers clenched. 'I don't know what you're talking about,' she answered, clearly trying, but failing, to keep distress out of her voice. 'If you don't stop threatening me I'll call the police.'

Sarah raised her hands slightly in a conciliatory manner. 'We're not threatening you. But I need to know where my sister is,' she stated emphatically. 'That's all. I'm not accusing you of anything.'

'You'd better not be, or you'll regret it,' Mari retorted, anger rising.

'Oh, you're threatening us now, are you?' Sarah raised her voice, frustration and fury welling again. Jennifer touched Sarah briefly on the shoulder, giving her an imploring look.

'Look,' said Jennifer steadily, 'we don't want any trouble. My friend is just trying to find her sister, Suzette. It's vital and you seem to know something. So please, will you help us?'

'We know Xavier Dubois has a connection with my sister,' continued Sarah, trying for calm. 'You know Dubois and someone called Suzette. All I want to know is where Suzette is,' she finished earnestly.

Mari answered coldly. 'I've already told your friend that I don't know Mr Dubois. I only met him this lunchtime. If he has any connection with your sister I wouldn't know anything about it.'

'But that's not true, is it? You spent a weekend with Dubois in Malvern.' In her frustration Sarah threw all remaining caution to the wind.

Mari reacted scathingly. 'I travel all over the country and meet lots of different clients and I often have dinner with them. I also work at the weekend sometimes. That's not a crime. Now get out of my way.'

Jennifer shook her head. 'But why say you only met Dubois today if you knew him already?'

'Because I'm not discussing my life with interfering strangers.'

Jennifer gripped Sarah's shoulder, hoping she'd back off to regroup, fearing they were putting themselves in danger, but Sarah ploughed on.

'Tell me where Suzette is!' she shrieked. People turned and looked.

Mari turned the ignition, put the car in gear and drove forward five metres. Sarah, balancing on her haunches, fell backwards onto the paving. 'I'm calling the police,' yelled Mari, before closing the car door and screeching out of the car park.

Chapter Fourteen

Sarah and Jennifer sat in Sarah's car discussing what had happened and what they might do next. Jennifer quietly took her friend's hand and they sat motionless for a short while.

'It feels like I can almost touch her,' Sarah spoke softly, her eyes still closed. She extended her other hand, fingers splayed. 'If I reach out my fingers… into the blackness… I can almost feel her fingertips. It's as if there's a connection but it's just beyond my grasp.' Sarah took a deep breath and wiped a tear from her cheek. At length she opened her eyes and shook her head slightly. 'We should know one another intimately. We share a joint identity and that's been stolen from us. I must find her. I have to.'

Jennifer squeezed her hand. 'You're doing brilliantly. In less than a month you've discovered that you have a twin, that she's not dead, contrary to what your parents have told you. And you an idea of who's involved. You will find her. We'll all help; you don't have to do any of this alone.'

Jennifer's words were comforting; however, the reassurance was short-lived. 'You know Jen, I'm fucking incensed at my parents telling me she died.' Sarah's tone was infused with bitterness and rage. 'I mean, why the hell would they do that?'

Jennifer shrugged, moving her head slowly from side to side. Knowing Jake and Lena well, it was incomprehensible to her. 'I'm sure they thought it was for the best, for whatever reason. They've always done their best for you.'

'Huh,' Sarah grunted. 'Who would lie about that to their child for Christ's sake? I can accept parents not telling a toddler, but why lie to an adult, years later? It makes my blood boil every time I think about it, which is pretty much all the time.'

'Well, when she was taken, perhaps they thought she had died,' Jennifer suggested tentatively.

'Then why wasn't there a police investigation?'

'We don't know there wasn't,' Jennifer responded gently. 'We simply know that it wasn't reported in the press. Maybe there was an undisclosed investigation by the police because it needed to be kept out of the public eye to protect you and your parents.'

'I suppose that's a possible explanation,' Sarah grudgingly concurred. 'I don't want to contact the police yet. I'd like to think there's some external pressure on Mum and Dad not to reveal that Suzette is alive. I mean, I'd feel better about them if they were prevented from speaking the truth. But God knows what the reason could be.'

'It's at least plausible. Perhaps they're protecting Suzette. Or maybe they were told she'd died and prevented from reporting it.'

'D'you think there was a cover up? It's something Ben and I discussed.'

Jennifer nodded. 'Possibly.' Her face wore a grave expression. 'There's a scenario that I've been thinking about.'

'What?' Sarah reacted apprehensively.

'Maybe your parents were involved, let's say, in a cover up. And if that was the case, it implies either they were part of whatever happened or they found out and were then blackmailed,' Jennifer offered cautiously. 'Goodness knows why but it's another potential explanation for why they've never said anything.'

'Ben and I talked about blackmail when we assumed Suzette was dead. My parents have never been wealthy, so we ruled out a ransom threat.'

'If not for a ransom, then blackmail might work if your parents were threatened to keep quiet for the sake of the child's safety but, having said that, most people would do almost anything to get their child back and would involve the police.' Jennifer paused. 'Unless Lena and Jake did something… terrible. I mean, I suppose the blackmail scenario would make sense if your mum and dad were… implicated.'

Sarah heaved a despairing sigh and thought for a few moments, her head in her hands. Then she turned to her friend, her countenance saturated with anguish. 'We ought to be considering why Suzette? Whatever the reason Mum and Dad haven't told the truth, it doesn't explain why Dubois abducted my sister. What if my parents were witness to a terrible crime and the kidnap of Suzette was a warning from the criminals not to speak out, or else they'd come back for me?'

Jennifer laid a consoling hand on Sarah's arm. 'If that's the case, your mum and dad are protecting you after all. You know,' she said after a pensive pause, 'we haven't considered that you might have all been placed into a witness protection scheme. Perhaps a criminal investigation was undertaken but Suzette wasn't found.'

'Witness protection?' Sarah considered it then shook her head. 'That doesn't seem likely to me. I'm pretty sure we've been in Malvern ever since Ullapool; don't people in that situation have to keep moving around?'

'I don't know, Sarah,' Jennifer sighed. 'It's just an idea. Your parents are originally from Plymouth, right? Maybe their and Dubois' paths crossed years ago.'

Despite her angst, Sarah managed a wry smile. 'I don't expect living in Plymouth in the '80s was exactly Miami Vice.'

Her amusement was fleeting, soon replaced by alarm. She turned to Jennifer, her hazel eyes widening. 'What if they're keeping her somewhere? What if she's been locked away all these years?'

Jennifer leaned over and gave her friend a big hug, speaking reassuringly and stroking her back. 'Hey, don't think the worst. There's no way it sounded like she's a prisoner. When Mari saw you in Malvern, I think she was simply asking you whether you were in Malvern with Dubois. That implies freedom, doesn't it?'

Sarah nodded. 'Sorry. I'm all over the place. But we've got to find her, Jen. God knows what kind of life she has; these people are criminals. Someone who could kidnap a child is probably capable of all sorts of things.'

'You've got to stay positive,' Jennifer continued, 'use your cool head, you're the analyst. It's me that's supposed to be the scatty one, remember?'

Sarah took a deep breath. 'You're right. Let's take this step by step.' She ran her fingers through her spikey hair, rubbing her head vigorously. 'Okay, so we're guessing

Suzette could be in England or France; probably France since Mari spoke to me in French.'

'That makes sense as Dubois is involved,' Jennifer agreed. 'But your online searches for her under his surname came up with nothing.'

'Yes, and I searched under Mari's surname, Thomas, and also drew a blank.' Sarah sat back in her seat, drumming the steering wheel with one finger.

Jennifer became engrossed in her phone, speedily swiping and tapping. 'I think you should seriously think about making a formal request to the police to know whether there was an investigation, given you're family. I would think it can be done confidentially and without you having to give much away at this stage. Here look,' she turned the screen to Sarah, 'you can request it under the Freedom of Information Act. It takes twenty days to get an initial response.'

Sarah stroked her lips with a finger while deliberating. At length she said resignedly, 'Yep, you're probably right. I'll look into it.'

Jennifer gave her an empathetic smile.

Sarah endeavoured to summon some galvanising positivity from deep within. 'Okay, what's our next move today? I don't think we'll get anything more from Marigold Thomas and we don't want the police after us for harassment. I think we should find the clinic where Dr Marchand works.' She retrieved her phone from its holder on the dashboard then located a clinic near Plymouth's large hospital to the north of the city. Next, she cross-checked with LinkedIn to see if she could find a Pierre Marchand connected to the clinic.

'Got him,' she stated after a minute or so, gratified.

'Isn't technology wonderful?' remarked Jennifer, smiling. 'However did our parents cope without mobiles and the Internet?'

'Yeah, but we're so used to the whole world being at our fingertips; technology can be bloody frustrating when your searches don't produce results.' She looked back at her screen for a few seconds. 'But in this case, we've hit the mark. Look, it appears Pierre Marchand works in fertility treatment. So d'you think we should try and speak with him?'

'He did seem pally with Dubois. Judging by all the hugging, their relationship appeared closer than simply consultant and client. I think it's definitely worth a try, but we'll have to be careful.'

Sarah concurred. 'If he knows Dubois well, he probably knows Suzette or has heard of her. Marigold mentioned Pierre during her phone call and said "we'll all have to be careful".' A thought occurred and she hit the steering wheel with both hands. 'Jeez! Marchand is involved in fertility treatment and that often leads to twins, doesn't it? So, supposing Suzette and I are the results of fertility treatment and Dubois got to know about us through his association with Marchand. Then, for whatever reason, say because he wanted a child of his own, he kidnapped Suzette. Maybe Marchand provided him with our details.'

Jennifer pondered this. 'It's possible he could have obtained information from Marchand, I guess. But why would he wait until you were toddlers? And it doesn't explain why your parents said your sister was dead, or many of the other things we've discussed,' she reasoned. 'Unless they had a hand in it,' she ended sadly. 'But I just don't see them doing that,' she added quickly, in a brighter tone.

Sarah reflected. 'What are you thinking of exactly when you say, "had a hand in it"?' she heard herself ask warily, immediately wishing she hadn't. She was afraid Jen's reply might echo thoughts she'd rather weren't materialised.

The expression on her friend's face confirmed Sarah's suspicion but Jennifer was already trying to dismiss the notion. 'They wouldn't. Sarah, they couldn't have…'

'Sold her, you mean? Jesus, I hope not,' she said, slowly shaking her head incredulously.

'No,' Jennifer affirmed, 'it might offer an explanation for why they may not have tried to find her and why they told you she was dead, but I can't believe your mum and dad capable of anything highly illegal, let alone selling their own child.'

Sarah turned to Jennifer, tears flooding her freckles. 'But we both had the same thought, didn't we? I couldn't possibly have doubted them a month ago. Now I just… don't know what to think.'

During their discussion, a myriad of emotions crashed through Sarah's mind and body, huge breakers foaming and splashing relentlessly one after the other, leaving her almost gasping for air and clutching any notion that crossed her mind. She realised she had to calm down in order to think rationally. Having taken a few moments to still herself, a weariness descended and she looked to her friend for direction.

'What shall we do then? Shall we put the postcode of the clinic in the satnav?'

'I think we have to,' Jennifer replied. 'Just one thing,'

she announced, buckling up, 'I'll do the talking and you stay in the car in case Dubois appears.'

Sarah heaved a sigh. 'Jen, I don't want to put you in any danger either. The chances are Ms Thomas has already told him of her encounter with us and if she hasn't, I bet she soon will. She knows what we both look like.'

'Yes, but she's no idea who I am or where we live. We have no reason to believe Dr Marchand knows anything about any of this and he's supposed to be in a meeting with Dubois right now. So if we get there quickly, I might be able to catch him straight afterwards.'

Sarah laid a hand on her friend's arm. 'But Marigold encountered me in Malvern, so she could assume either I live there or have some connection with the place. And although she has no idea who you are, she could easily trace both of us through social media. So please think carefully. Do you really want to do this? I'm already deeply involved but you don't have to be. If we are close to the truth, who knows what any of them might do to stop us.'

Jennifer placed her hand on Sarah's. 'I'm doing this,' she stated emphatically.

'Okay, Jen, but if you happen to see Dubois, don't approach him directly about Suzette. We don't know how dangerous he is or what he has to lose. Hearing a description of someone and seeing them yourself are not the same. If he's not seen you and you're not pursuing him, he has no reason to come after you. You have Emily and Adam to think about,' Sarah warned.

'You have a family too.'

'Yes, but I'm the one with the missing sister, so I get to call the shots. Besides, I promised Ben we wouldn't do anything rash.'

Jennifer reached onto the back seat. 'I'd better wear this then,' she grinned, donning Ben's cap and dispersing the tension. It went perfectly with her long hair. 'At least I can shield my face from security cameras.

Sarah gave a quiet snort, raised her eyebrows and nodded. 'You look good in that,' she admitted, smiling, 'better than me.'

'Better than Ben?' teased Jennifer.

'Almost.' Sarah managed a chuckle.

Within twenty minutes they had found the clinic and parked the car a little way down the road.

'Don't forget, keep texting,' urged Sarah, leaning across the passenger seat to speak before Jennifer shut the door.

It seemed an age before Sarah received the first text. "Waiting in reception. Marchand in a meeting". Another thirty minutes went by before the next text appeared. "He's coming down the stairs…"

Jennifer watched through the chic steel staircase's glass side panels as a group of eight businessmen and women descended. To her relief Dubois was not among them. However, Pierre Marchand led the assembly into the spacious modern reception area. He shook each of them warmly by the hand and wished them well on their respective journeys. Jennifer was sitting on one of four large comfy leather sofas positioned around a glass table on which lay a few brochures and other magazines. During her forty-minute stay several couples arrived and left, some shown into other parts of the building. Intermittently the receptionist had asked Jennifer if she still wanted to wait, as it wasn't clear how long the meeting would go on. Jennifer had noted where the security camera was and sat with her back to it, leafing through the information on the table.

It was clear Dr Marchand was the director of the clinic and he seemed to have an excellent reputation judging by the information Jennifer had uncovered online. His substantial publication list spanned three decades, focussing on the causes and treatment of infertility and in-vitro fertilisation techniques. It seemed to Jennifer, who knew nothing about medical research, that much of Marchand's was at the cutting edge, judging by the use of words such as 'novel', 'innovative' and 'pioneering' in the papers' titles, but she supposed all published research must push the boundaries of understanding. There were many scientific terms she didn't understand. The glossy brochures on the table mainly offered IVF services.

Pierre Marchand's tall slim frame appeared in front of her, offering her his hand. Jennifer stood and cleared her throat nervously. She hoped that he couldn't hear the blood rushing through her ears as her heart thumped wildly.

'Dr Marchand. I believe you wanted to see me. 'Ow can I 'elp?' He smiled politely, his tanned skin momentarily creasing around his eyes and mouth.

'Um, yes, J…' Jennifer paused, 'Julia. Julia Beecham. Thank you for seeing me without an appointment.'

'Please.' Marchand indicated Jennifer should sit again, seating himself on an adjacent sofa. His hazel eyes seemed to bore into hers, making her slightly uncomfortable.

Jennifer's mouth was dry. She took a sip of water from the paper cup obtained from a nearby vending machine. 'I haven't come to discuss medical treatment.'

'Oh?'

'No. You see I have a friend who I lost touch with a while back and I think I saw her today from a distance. I called after her, but she didn't hear me and drove off before I could reach her.'

'I see. What does this 'ave to do with me?' Marchand interjected politely, his face as unreadable as blank paper.

'Well, I also saw a man I recognised as a friend of hers from one of the photos she'd sent me. That man was having lunch with you. I don't know him, but the barman knew you and I thought maybe if you're friends with her friend you might know her.' Jennifer's explanation trailed off and she shrugged hesitantly.

The corners of Marchand's mouth twitched slightly. 'If I understand you correctly, you're asking me if I know the friend of the man I 'ad lunch with.'

'Yes, that's right.'

He shrugged nonchalantly. 'What is 'er name, your friend?'

'Oh of course, silly me.' Jennifer felt flustered. There was something about this man that unnerved her. She hoped that the manner he reserved for his patients was more calming. 'It's Suzette.'

'Well,' he straightened his back in preparation for standing, 'I'm afraid I don't know a Suzette,' he replied matter-of-factly. 'The man I 'ad lunch with is a business colleague. I don't know 'im that well.' He stood and extended his hand again. 'Sorry to disappoint you.'

Jennifer got to her feet. 'You seemed to know him quite well. Do you hug all your business colleagues?' she blurted.

He studied her for a moment. *Shit*, she thought, *I've gone too far.*

At length he shrugged again and shook his head

slightly. 'It's 'ow we French do things; simply good business,' he answered dispassionately.

At that moment a tall burly man in a sharp suit walked across the reception and handed Marchand a small piece of paper. He nodded his thanks, glanced at the note, then at Jennifer, before folding and pocketing it. Then he turned and walked back up the stairs.

Chapter Fifteen

Sarah and Jennifer waited an hour or so in the back lane behind the tall pale green and white house, the destination of Pierre Marchand's Maserati. They'd only observed one person in the car but, as Sarah had pointed out, it would have been simple to conceal another. Jennifer wasn't sure they should be there. She'd known as she'd left the clinic her story hadn't been believed. They weren't used to this; a professional investigator would do a better job.

Sarah eventually agreed they could do no more that evening. No one else had left or entered the house from the back. They decided to go to their bed and breakfast. Sarah had made a note of the address and would talk with Andy Finch about investigating Dubois and Marchand further through the public records.

Over a bolognaise supper and a bottle of Sangiovese they reviewed the situation. Jennifer was to fly from Exeter to Newcastle then take the train to York the following morning. Sarah revealed she'd booked two flights from Birmingham to Bergerac the coming Saturday. She explained she'd learned from Dubois' assistant from which airport and on what date Dubois would return to France and had investigated flights from Birmingham to Rouen or Cahors, where Équipé Pharmaceuticals was based. There were no flights to either location, however, she'd found a flight to Bergerac, an hour and forty minutes' drive from Cahors. Since she knew that Dubois was based in Cahors, she'd made an educated guess he'd be on that flight. She'd talked it over with Ben and he'd forbidden her to go alone, admitting that, although he wasn't comfortable with her plan to track Dubois, he knew she wouldn't back down, so he'd agreed to go too, with the proviso they keep Jen and Adam informed of their whereabouts.

'Dubois will be travelling on the Sunday, so Ben and I will go a day earlier so we can hire a car and be ready to shadow him when he arrives,' she told Jennifer.

The following morning, having dropped Jennifer at Exeter airport, Sarah drove home. The sky was dreary with low cloud and persistent rain. During the journey recent conversations played repeatedly in her mind. She hadn't tried to contact her parents again. Since they'd lied to her, she'd decided there was no point in asking any further questions until they returned and at the moment, she couldn't even think of them without fury and resentment. *With or without them I'll get to the bottom of this if it kills me*, she thought, quickly resolving not to tempt fate with ominous thoughts, then dismissing that notion as unscientific.

She recalled what Moira said: *Suzy didnae die in Ullapool. It was strange the way yer mum left suddenly. Suzy,* Sarah thought; not *Suzette*. She felt a familiarity, a connection, with the name Suzy that she hadn't experienced with Suzette and rolled the name in her mind; *Suzy, Suzy.* The word began to morph subliminally into the comforting sound 'Ouzi'. A rush of adrenalin arose as she suddenly remembered as a young child having an imaginary friend called Ouzi. Realisation dawned; for several years after Suzette's disappearance she'd been trying to communicate with her lost sister.

Malvern, England, 1 June 2018

Sarah spent much of Friday morning in the office catching up on email correspondence. At eleven she was interrupted by a call from reception. Their administrator was irritated, saying she'd put Sarah's visitor in the Elgar conference room—she was lucky it was available—and reminding her to book guests in. She put the phone down before Sarah could ask the name of her unexpected caller.

Sarah opened the door to the meeting room to find a tall, dark-suited woman, with reddish-grey hair closely layered around her angular face. She was not smiling. Sarah glanced at her quizzically then, remembering her manners, stepped forward, hand outstretched. 'Sarah Lester. How can I help you?'

The woman shook her hand briefly, fixing her with an unnerving stare through solemn grey eyes. She spoke in a collected, formal tone. 'Miss Lester, I'm here in a legal capacity, representing my client Ms Thomas. I understand you've been involved in two incidents of harassment of my client and I'm here to give you an informal warning. I'm sure you understand that harassment can be a criminal offence under the Protection from Harassment Act 1997.'

Taken aback, Sarah struggled for some moments to speak, a tide of apprehension restricting her throat.

The woman continued. 'My client was very clear in her instruction. She would prefer not to take this further, however she will pursue a court action to obtain an injunction against you if there are any further occurrences; that is to say if you approach her again.'

As her anger rose, Sarah fought to remain calm, thoughts buzzing. She felt outraged at the unfairness of the situation. She was the innocent party. This solicitor spouting legal threats knew nothing of the actual circumstances. She had to counter the accusation but how far should she go? What exactly could she say?

She stepped forward, taking hold of the back of a conference chair to steady herself. 'I can only guess at what Marigold Thomas has said,' she responded curtly. 'I wasn't harassing her. In fact Ms Thomas approached me when we first encountered one another. She clearly thought I was my twin sister, who, crucially, is missing. Then she denied all knowledge of her.'

'Ms Thomas has apprised me fully of the details,' the solicitor retorted in her unswerving official tone. 'She mistook you for someone else. People mistake persons for individuals they know all the time.'

'It's obvious she knows Suzette; she mentioned her name,' Sarah persisted.

'You are incorrect. The name Ms Thomas spoke, Soubrette, is not the same as that of your sister. In any case that is irrelevant and does not provide a justification for pursuing her, as you have done.'

'I'm trying to find my sister; she's missing, for God's sake. Marigold Thomas knows something. She can't blame me for asking her about Suzette; for trying to get her to talk to me. I'm sure you'd do the same in my position.'

'You have caused her distress on two separate occasions. You followed her, tried to restrain her, threatened her and prevented her from departing. As I said, harassment can be a criminal offence. Do you really want a criminal charge levied against you?'

With frustration threatening to overwhelm her, all Sarah wanted was to scream at this woman; to tell her the whole story, lay everything bare, accuse her client of possible illegal involvement in her sister's disappearance, or at least a cover up, which she believed amounted to the same thing. But what actual proof did she have?

Then she realised the woman was asking her a question.

'Miss Lester, I repeat, do you understand? Or you will find yourself with an injunction, at best, or subject to prosecution.'

Sarah thought a moment then replied slowly, 'How did you find me? How do you know who I am?'

'That is immaterial.'

'But it's not, is it?'

The woman's countenance remained impassive.

'I didn't catch your name.'

'I didn't give it. As I said, I'm acting legally for Ms Thomas.'

'How well do you know Marigold Thomas? What did she actually tell you?' Sarah continued evenly, her tone belying the thumping in her chest. 'She obviously knows who I am and how's that I wonder? I didn't tell her my name, yet here you are, turning up at my place of work.'

The solicitor's tone changed from uncompromising to hostile. 'I've given you a warning. There won't be another. I suggest you stay away from my client or there will be consequences.' The woman turned and stepped towards the door then looked back at Sarah. 'Consider those you love.'

Then she was gone.

At the woman's last words, alarm gripped Sarah and held her captive. It was minutes before she could move, hours before she was able to function effectively again.

Sarah arrived home late that afternoon to find Ben packing his rucksack. He'd placed a small holdall on their bed for her things.

'What's the matter?' he asked concernedly.

She told him about her encounter. As she did so, slowly but surely, determination began to replace her anxiety.

Ben listened quietly until she relayed the woman's last remark. 'Shit! They're threatening not only you but your parents and me too! Sarah, you should take this warning seriously. These people seem like professionals, they know what they're doing. We don't know what we're getting into and it sounds pretty heavy.'

'It was always going to be,' retorted Sarah heatedly. 'Kidnap is a serious offence. It's obvious Dubois and his gang are trying to frighten me off.' She drew herself up to her full height. 'Well, I won't be intimidated,' she stated resolutely. 'They can fuck off. I'm going to find my sister, whatever it takes!'

'They know who you are and where you work, so they'll know where we live and I'm sure they'll be able to find your parents too. You've obviously touched a nerve. They're threatening you because you've become a threat to them. Perhaps you should talk to Jake and Lena again now. They're obviously involved. Ask them. They might know something that will help you find her.' Ben's response was cautious and calm, a sure sign to Sarah that she was beginning to dig her heels in with a 'come what may' attitude.

'We've been over this,' she answered angrily. 'They've already lied to me multiple times. Why wouldn't they simply lie to me again? I can't trust them, Ben, and I know you don't either. Anyway, if they have been intimidated in the past and they did whatever they had to do to protect us, don't you think they'd just carry on doing it? Especially as I've now been warned off. They wouldn't tell me the truth, even if they did answer my calls—which they're not doing. The only way I'm going to find Suzy is by tracking Dubois.'

'Okay, okay,' Ben yielded. 'You're right. We can't trust your folks.' He moved to the window and Sarah followed his gaze. There was no sign of the sun in the leaden sky and dark clouds, heavy with rain, were gathering to the east. 'Dubois has been clever. I mean, you don't have any formal written warning to take to the police. In fact, when it all boils down what can you actually prove? They're obviously sufficiently agitated to be trying to deter you but they're in a strong position.' He turned to look at her. 'We don't know what they're capable of.'

'Yeah, I know.' Sarah sank onto the bed. 'I'm aware all the evidence is circumstantial. But the pieces add up: the fact that Marigold Thomas engaged a solicitor implies she has something to hide; the fact that she denied knowing Dubois when she is clearly close to him; the foreign men asking questions about my parents in Ullapool just after they moved without warning; my childhood memory of Dubois. There's no doubt in my mind. Dubois will lead us to Suzette.'

Ben heaved a reluctant sigh. 'I suppose if we pursue

Dubois in France, we're not following Marigold and we can't be subject to a UK court action.' He ran his hands through his curls and scratched his head vigorously while thinking. 'Okay, let's do this. But we're checking in with Jen and Adam every hour we're over there. Any trouble and we go to the police. Fuck knows what your parents may or may not have got themselves involved in. Now we're opening ourselves up to whatever it is.'

Sarah closed her eyes momentarily with relief. She would have gone alone but felt infinitely safer with Ben by her side. She moved towards Ben and gave him a hug. 'Thank you,' she said earnestly, 'it means a lot.'

He kissed the top of her head, inhaling her warmth. 'Come on, we'd better get packing.'

Chapter Sixteen

Bergerac, France, 2 June 2018

By the time Sarah and Ben had landed in Bergerac, wound their way through the hot poky shed that served as a terminal for immigration and collected their hired Peugeot, it was the middle of the afternoon. Ben had booked their hotel for the night but hadn't told Sarah where they would be staying. She was glad he'd taken care of it, as her mind couldn't seem to accommodate anything other than the focus of their trip.

To her surprise they drove south, away from the town. Seeing her worried look, Ben reassured her. 'Don't worry, it's not far. We'll be able to get back to the airport easily tomorrow morning. I found a place that should be peaceful, where we can chill out before tomorrow. I think it will be relaxing—just what you could do with.'

Sarah returned his tender smile. 'You always know what I need; sometimes better than I do myself.'

They crossed a wide, gently rolling plane dotted with isolated groups of trees, the road leading them between sweeping vineyards, past solitary stone farmhouses and the occasional winery offering *Dégustation Gratuite,* through tiny hamlets and past a number of burgundy signs indicating directions to nearby chateaus.

After a few kilometres the road rose gradually until they came to the outskirts of a hilltop village. To their right was an old covered *lavoir* sited over a spring; to their left a church with a distinctive bell-gable, its creamy-yellow limestone walls glowing in the soft afternoon light. Rounding a bend they reached the village square with a stone-flagged marketplace bounded by square pillars supporting a red-brown pan-tile roof. A few shops bordered the square: a bakery, a grocer and a *tabac*. There was also a café bar, outside which sat several men of varying ages enjoying conversation and the sunshine. A large black Labrador was sleeping in the shade next to the café entrance. The remainder of the old stone buildings were two- and three-storey houses with white shutters, a few with ornate metal balconies on the second floor.

Ben pulled up momentarily to look at his phone then, having located the hotel, drove around the square and down a small side street. The small auberge was located at the edge of the village. He swung the car into a parking space in an open-sided barn to one side of the pebbled courtyard. The ends of the barn were hardly visible under a huge rambling pink clematis.

'Ben, it's beautiful,' Sarah exclaimed.

The sizeable sandy limestone building incorporated three levels, the tiny windows of the top floor being set in the roof. To one end was a four-storey *pigeonnier*, now converted to domestic space. Merlot-coloured wooden shutters adorned the windows and a set of stone steps with attractive iron railings led to one of the second-floor balconies, which was fringed with clay pots containing a variety of spring flowers. A magnificent purple wisteria clambered over the walls.

They entered through a wide door into a sunlit reception area leading onto a long, cosy lounge which accommodated a couple of comfy-looking sofas. Several large cinnamon-coloured rugs lay on the travertine floor. Antique chairs and small tables hugged the walls and an imposing dark wooden dresser stood in one corner. The light from table lamps, supplementing the sunlight, reflected off white-painted wooden ceiling beams, affording the room a pretty glow.

The proprietor, a woman in her fifties, slender, dark-haired and with kind eyes, welcomed them in French. Ben's French was almost non-existent as he'd had no interest in paying attention at school. Sarah understood a few words. Having studied a phrasebook on the flight, she tried to say that they'd booked a double room for one night and to ask the woman to reply slowly, however muddled some of the words.

Hearing their difficulty, the lady grinned, replying in perfect English. "Ello, I'm Rachelle. What is your family name please?'

Ben sighed with relief. 'Ah, you speak English! Thank you. Sorry that we're so bad at speaking French. I'm Ben Tayoh and this is Sarah Lester. I booked the room under my name.' He passed Rachelle their passports, then looked around at Sarah and smiled.

Sarah liked hearing Ben use his surname as, unlike most people, he'd chosen it himself. In his mid-twenties, desperate to shake off his unhappy and unproductive youth, Ben had changed his last name by deed poll. He'd constructed a name that sounded phonetically like one of his favourite rugby players. After that, according to Ben, he was finally able to become the person he wanted to be, shedding his insecurities and controlling the flashes of temper that blighted his former years, channelling his aggression through sport. Once Sarah met him he'd managed to put away his beginnings, sustaining only the positive aspects of his character, and was making new, happy memories. Sarah appreciated that this had been difficult and greatly admired him for it. The only negative was that he always had to spell 'Tayoh' for people.

Rachelle showed them to their room at the top of the *pigeonnier* via three narrow twisting staircases and several wooden-floored corridors furnished with *chaise longues* and traditional old French tables.

Their room was bright, painted apple white, with a balcony overlooking lush vineyards and a small pasture dotted with sheep. An attractive metal-framed bed was positioned to take advantage of the view from a smaller window. Dark oak rafters showed beneath the apex of the roof, which was sympathetically insulated and boarded between the beams. A small shower room had been carved out of the space at one end.

Sarah threw open the door to the balcony and stepped out. A round table and two chairs nestled against the wall under a rambling grapevine. The heady scent of wisteria hung in the warm air. On the table stood a bottle of Bergerac and two glasses with a handwritten note: *Bienvenue.*

Ben popped his head around the door to check Sarah's expression, which was full of surprise and delight. He nodded towards the wine. 'I called ahead,' he smiled.

Sarah turned to him, the gold and green hues of her eyes glistening, and threw her arms around him. 'I love you so much.'

'Love you too. We don't know what tomorrow will bring, so let's immerse ourselves in this evening and enjoy it.'

After a stroll around the village they returned to the auberge, ordered a supper of cheeses with a walnut salad and warm French bread and sat on the balcony, enjoying this taste of France and drinking wine in the golden glow of the early evening sunlight.

Later that night they made love gently and purposefully, taking time over each tender kiss, exploring one another as if it was the first time, except that they each knew where to linger, how to elicit the most exquisite responses with the smallest movement. They enabled their loving to endure, desisting at specific moments, prolonging the rise, the yearning for ultimate satisfaction.

They slept curled, foetus-like, Ben's arm protectively around Sarah's waist.

'Whatever happens, I'll keep you safe,' he murmured.

Sunday dawned with a clear sky. Lucent white curtains sighing gently in the warm breeze muted the rising sun, affording the room a pure light. Ben and Sarah breakfasted early on warm croissants with jam, fresh orange juice and strong coffee. By eight-thirty they were on the road back to Bergerac airport. There were a couple of flights arriving from Birmingham that day and the first was due to land around nine. They didn't speak much, anxiety having set in, but each comforted the other with gestures: a kiss, a squeeze of the hand, a pat on the arm. They were in this situation together and they shared the burden. They'd agreed to pursue Dubois and discreetly enquire into the whereabouts of Suzette from anyone he seemed to know well. However, if circumstances turned nasty or dangerous they would retreat and return home. They'd arranged to text Jen and Adam hourly. They hadn't agreed a threshold for what constituted danger—Sarah suspected her interpretation would be less restrictive than Ben's, but he'd sworn to protect her come what may.

A plane landed at ten past nine. Ben had parked the car in the short-stay car park under a large canopy incorporating solar panels. They had a view of the exit door from the arrivals section, albeit from some way off. They waited nervously. At about nine twenty-five people emerged. After a couple of minutes Dubois appeared in jeans and a casual white shirt, a jacket slung over his shoulder. He looked at his phone. Sarah gasped and grabbed the road map they'd purchased the previous day, spreading it between their faces and the windscreen. Given their height difference she couldn't see without Ben being visible, so Ben peered over the top of the paper, relaying Dubois' movements.

'He's walking to the ticket machine. He's on the phone, laughing. He's walking this way. He seems to be looking right at us.'

'Jesus.'

'No, I'm wrong, he's heading for the long-stay car park.' Ben opened his door.

'Where are you going?'

'I'm going to have to get out to see which car he's getting into.'

'Don't let him see you.'

Ben walked a few paces from the car, returning quickly. 'He's in a metallic blue Porsche 911. Get ready to follow our location on your phone.'

'At least his car is easy to spot. Hopefully there are loads of grey Peugeots around.' Sarah tried to sound cheerful though her heart was racing.

'Okay, here we go.' Ben pulled out of the car park. The Porsche was two cars ahead on the airport exit road.

The speed limit was restricted for the first kilometre or so, allowing Ben to adjust to the hire car again. Thereafter the Porsche sped up, nudging over the maximum speed limit. Ben had no choice but to follow, praying they wouldn't be stopped. After a further kilometre Dubois made a left turn onto another main road signposted Issigeac. After about ten minutes, as they neared the village, the road passed under a long avenue of beech trees. Cars were pulling into parking areas among the trees on either side of the road and the area was busy with people walking along the roadside carrying wicker baskets and woven bags, pushing buggies, restraining children and holding onto dogs. Dubois swung into a grassy parking area on the right, cruising up and down until he found a space. There was obviously something going on. Ben managed to find one of the last spaces, in the far corner, and they jumped out of the car. Sarah spotted Dubois making his way along the main road towards the village carrying a green canvas bag. They followed, donning sunglasses and keeping a safe distance.

They came upon an extensive area of medieval half-timbered buildings in a maze of narrow winding streets. The two- and three-storey buildings were furnished with coloured shutters bracketing old multi-paned windows; some possessed attractive shop fronts on the ground floor, others were residential and a few retained tiny balconies on the second floor. A bustling market was in progress with all manner of goods on sale from clothes and jewellery to bread and fish. The market wound through the streets, following their curves. The delightful place seemed an incongruous backdrop to the sinister situation they were embroiled in.

They had to make sure they didn't lose sight of Dubois in the multitude of market-goers. Luckily he was tall and Ben could see him among the mass of bobbing heads and colourful stalls. Dubois stopped at a cheese stall groaning with produce. Ben and Sarah pretended to be interested in a multi-coloured stand displaying olives and spices in large wooden bowls. The pungent aromas of garlic, turmeric, cinnamon and ginger filled their nostrils. Having purchased three pieces of cheese, Dubois was on the move again. Ben grabbed Sarah's hand to ensure they stayed together and they wove slowly through the crowd. Dubois had stopped at a charcuterie stand piled with dried sausages and other meats in wicker baskets. Long plaits of garlic hung from the canopy. Ben watched as Dubois chose a long, thin dark sausage and a short, plump one with a whitish skin. Having put the purchases in his bag, Dubois turned and looked up, seemingly straight at Ben, who bent his head to examine a jar of local honey on the adjacent stall. As they progressed through the market, turning this way and that, Dubois added salad ingredients and bread to his supplies, ending up at a rotisserie selling whole cooked chickens and pan-fried vegetables. The rich mixture of culinary aromas floating through the village triggered Sarah's appetite and, notwithstanding her apprehension, she'd taken the opportunity to buy a country loaf, some cured ham and a scoop of dried figs. At least they would have provisions for later which would survive in the warm weather.

'Ever practical,' Ben had smiled.

With his chicken and sliced garlic potatoes on board, Dubois stopped at a café bar in a busy square. Ben and Sarah hung back, unsure what to do. There was another eatery diagonally across the square next to an old church however the two establishments were in full view of one another.

As the sun continued to confer its warmth, its rays reaching down among the old houses, Sarah and Ben withdrew into the shade of the spacious stone arch at the entrance to the church. However, they couldn't easily see Dubois from their position, so Ben had to repeatedly peek around a buttress.

'I think we should get hats,' Sarah announced.

'What?'

'Hats. Look, there's a stall over there. We're wearing sunglasses like most people here; we could also wear hats. My hair is distinctive, so I should cover it. Dubois saw you in Malvern, so you need to be better disguised. Quite a few folk have hats on.'

Ben saw the stall selling bags, scarves and headgear at the end of a short alleyway next to the church. It wasn't visible from the café. 'Okay, good idea. You go first.'

Having found a flexible wide-brimmed cork hat for herself, Sarah relieved Ben of his watch. She pulled the brim down to shade her face and stood slightly away from the church, pretending to look at her phone. Every so often she glanced up briefly to check Dubois out of the corner of her eye. Dubois was drinking coffee. Ben returned with a baseball cap and a French newspaper. They spotted a couple about to leave the nearby bistro across the square from Dubois and occupied the seats as soon as they became vacant. Dubois now appeared to have a beer and a plate of something. They ordered cold drinks, settled half-hidden by the newspaper and waited.

Half an hour later, Ben popped into the café to answer a call of nature. The moment he left the table Sarah saw Dubois rise from his chair. Shit. What should she do? She glanced through the window, but Ben was nowhere to be seen. Dubois was shaking hands with someone and was about to leave. She made the decision to follow; she couldn't bear to lose him—for all she knew Suzette might be close by. She texted Ben saying she'd send him her location every minute until he caught up with her.

Dubois disappeared down a side street and Sarah ran across the square in time to see him make another turn. It was midday. A couple of the market traders were packing up but most stalls were still in full swing. She shadowed Dubois through a back lane leading away from the market. He turned again, through a narrow alleyway, then into a cobbled passageway under the upper floor of the adjacent houses. Sarah texted the name of the alley to Ben before glancing into the passage. Dubois had disappeared. Cautiously, she made her way over the cobbles. Her view was restricted but the passage seemed to be leading to a small courtyard. As she neared its exit, she could see two of the four houses enclosing the courtyard; each had its back to the others and possessed a small timber door and windows with closed shutters. Several terracotta pots planted with flowers were dotted around beside the walls. The opposite side of the yard was in full sun while the area in front of her was in shade.

Sarah stepped out of the passageway and immediately heard a low voice close to her ear, 'Fucking stop following me or I'll 'ave you arrested.'

Sarah's heart thumped and she felt sick with fear. She whipped around to see Dubois looming above her. His face radiated rage and his fists were clenched. She took several steps backwards.

'I just need to talk to you,' she said quickly. 'I'm not threatening you.'

'You could 'ave talked to me at the café,' Dubois retorted angrily, his dark brown eyes boring into hers. 'Why are you following me?'

'I'm trying to find my sister... and I think you know where she is,' Sarah responded shakily.

'You don't know me or anything about me. Why the 'ell should I know your sister?'

'I thought I knew your face... from a long time ago... and... your friend Mari, the one you had lunch with in Malvern... she thought I was Suzette and she mentioned your name—she said "have you come with Xavier".'

'You seem to know my face because you've been following me around. Do you think I'm stupid?' he yelled. 'You 'arassed my friend and you're 'arassing me. She's taken legal action. You were warned to stay away or there would be consequences. You understand? *Comprenez?*' He took a step forward.

Sarah didn't reply. She was trying to think, to play for time. Where the fuck was Ben?

'Well?' Dubois shouted furiously, walking towards her.

Sarah backed away but lost her footing on the uneven stones so that she tumbled, twisting her ankle. Her phone rang in her pocket. She gave a cry as she stumbled getting to her feet. Dubois had reached her. A sharp pain seared through bone and muscle as she tried to limp away from him and she cried out again.

'*Fils de pute,*' Dubois exclaimed. 'Stop,' he bellowed into her face.

As she attempted to regain her balance, Sarah assessed her options. Dubois was between her and the passageway; she couldn't easily walk let alone run; Ben would turn up at any minute; she might as well keep him talking. She repeated a single thought to herself; *he didn't kill her, so he's not going to kill me.* It was a flimsy theory but felt vaguely reassuring at that moment.

Shaking his head and staring at the ground, Dubois lowered his voice, 'Why the fuck did you 'ave to persist?' He resumed his scrutiny of her.

Her phone rang again but she was too afraid to answer it.

'Please, don't… hurt me. Can we just talk?'

Something passed across his face as he looked at her, perhaps a slight softening of his features, a hint of recognition in his eyes. Then the line of his mouth hardened again.

'I'm not going to 'urt you,' he responded testily. 'You're doing that all by yourself. Sit 'ere,' he motioned easing himself to the ground.

Tentatively relieved, she took the weight off her injured foot and sat cautiously a little way from him, considering how to proceed.

'When you look at me you see her,' she risked. 'We're identical, we're family. I have a right to know her.'

Dubois ran both hands over his face, clearly trying to think. At length, he heaved a frustrated sigh. 'You want to know about your sister?' he uttered bitterly. 'She's where she belongs and she's 'appy. You want to get that?' He gestured to her ringing pocket.

Sarah nodded and took the phone out with a shaking hand. She had three missed calls from Ben. She called back, hastily explained where she was and hung up. 'He'll be here any moment,' she lied, not knowing where exactly Ben was. She realised she must keep things calm if she was to learn any more. 'My twin sister disappeared before we were two years old,' she stated determinedly, looking at the cobblestones ahead of her. 'I want to know where she is.'

'What 'ave your parents told you?'

'They said she was dead.' Sarah tried to keep resentment from her voice.

'And why didn't you believe them?'

'There was no death certificate.'

'So why do you think I was involved?' Dubois spoke calmly.

Sarah didn't know how best to answer. She knew in her heart he'd kidnapped her sister but if she accused him he could take it as a threat and might still harm her. If it became clear that she had no evidence against him he could easily refuse to tell her anything. She could threaten him with an investigation, but she couldn't risk provoking him. 'I know about the fertility clinic,' she blurted.

He stared at her, swallowed, then his eyes narrowed. 'You 'aven't answered my last question.'

Sarah realised her words had resonated with him on some level, but she wasn't getting any nearer to knowing where Suzette was. She took a gamble. 'Can I trust you?'

Dubois shrugged. 'You 'ave to trust me or there is no

point to this conversation.'

'Okay, so you have to trust me too. I'm not here for any kind of accusation or retribution.' Sarah took a deep breath. The sun had moved around, reaching her feet. Her left ankle was throbbing. 'We were in the same café in Malvern nine days ago. I followed your friend Mari after she'd mistaken me for Suzette. I heard you on the telephone. It triggered… a memory.' She turned to face him. 'I saw you… in my bedroom… when I was a child. I saw you take her.'

Dubois was quiet for a moment or two. He stroked his greying beard then spoke ominously. 'You 'ave no idea what you 'ave stepped into. Things aren't always as they seem, you know. You should listen to your parents, forget what you think you saw. People's realities can be quite different from one another's. Your sister is well and she is 'appy. She 'as 'er life and you 'ave yours. Do you want to ruin that?'

'I don't want to ruin anything,' Sarah retorted sharply, 'but the truth is important. Don't you think she has a right to know that she has a twin?'

'Oh, and what do you think would 'appen then?' Dubois responded angrily. 'Did you intend to waltz into 'er life, tell 'er she's your sister and play 'appy families? You from England and 'er in France; you don't think there'd be questions? She's where she belongs, living a contented life with 'er 'usband. You want to come in and blow all that apart?' Dubois' voice was rising heatedly. 'Go 'ome. Go back to your own life and be 'appy!'

Sarah shook her head. 'I can't.'

He moved towards her suddenly, placing a hand on her arm. She detected a note of entreatment in his tone. 'It would be worse for you, much worse, not to mention your parents, believe me. Why do you think they lied to you? To protect you. If you know what's good for you, forget all about this.'

'I can't simply forget I have a twin sister,' she exclaimed.

At that moment Ben came storming through the alleyway. Seeing Sarah on the ground with Dubois he leapt towards them, fists curled ready to strike the back of her attacker's head. Simultaneously, Sarah cried, 'Ben!' and Dubois let go of her arm, turning around, raising his palms defensively.

'Let her go,' Ben yelled. 'Don't you touch her or I'll fucking kill you.'

'Stop, Ben. It's okay, I'm okay,' Sarah urged.

Dubois scrambled to his feet. Spreading his hands towards Ben in a pacifying gesture, he spoke insistently, 'I'm not 'urting 'er.'

The two men eyed one another, head-to-head. Although the Frenchman was fit and strong for a man his age—Sarah guessed he was in his late fifties—she knew Ben could take him and sensed Dubois knew it too.

'Ben, we were only talking,' Sarah exhorted.

Ben unclenched his hands and dropped his arms. 'Didn't look like it.' He stared at his would-be opponent threateningly.

Dubois ran his hands through his hair. 'We should go somewhere else and talk,' he said resignedly. He looked at Sarah. 'Your foot needs attention.'

'Sarah, are you injured? What's wrong?' Ben rushed to her and crouched by her side protectively.

'I've twisted my ankle, that's all.'

'Come on, let's get you up.' Ben placed his right arm around her back and under her right shoulder, supporting her left arm with his. Dubois took a step towards them to help but Ben barked, 'Stay away.' With bent knees, he took Sarah's weight and stood up, dragging her with him.

'Can you walk?'

'I think so.'

Sarah took a step forward but as soon as she put weight on the injured ankle she felt an intense sharp pain and yelped involuntarily.

'Let me 'elp, for Christ's sake,' Dubois uttered. 'There's a café around the corner.'

Ben nodded his consent. Both men supporting Sarah, they slowly made their way out of the courtyard.

Chapter Seventeen

They sat at a round metal table outside an old-style teashop in a quiet courtyard bathed in sunlight. Large turquoise umbrellas protected the tables and their occupants from the heat. An old red-brick wall six feet high ran along one side, purple aubrieta spilling from its apex and tumbling over the rough surface, gaining new holds in manifold crevices. Further along a pale pink clematis clambered rampantly over the brickwork, its delicate, scented flowers attracting numerous bees.

Dubois ordered wine and water for the table. Sarah didn't feel like eating but knew she would have to consume something to take a painkiller. The lunchtime special was warm mushroom quiche with salad and rosemary-roasted potatoes and they decided on that. Sarah sat with her damaged foot on Ben's lap, gritting her teeth as he checked for broken bones.

'No breaks, just a twist.'

'Thank Christ for that,' responded Sarah, bending her leg to put her foot down.

Ben stopped her. 'Best to keep it up for a bit,' he advised.

A waiter brought wine and water and took their food order. Ben pulled the water jug across the table. Scooping up the floating ice cubes, he wrapped them in a napkin and applied it to the swollen tissue around Sarah's ankle. 'Ideally you need compression, but this will have to do.'

'I can 'elp,' stated Dubois gruffly. He entered the café and after a couple of minutes came out with a plastic bag of crushed ice. 'Wrap this around it.' He looked at his watch. 'The pharmacy will close in fifteen minutes; I'll get you a bandage.'

Ben placed a hand on Dubois' arm. 'How do we know you won't disappear?'

Dubois sighed and shook his head. 'As I said, you 'ave to trust me or this won't work.' Seeing the look of suspicion on Ben's face he reached into his pocket and placed a car key on the table attached to a black leather fob bearing a metal shield presenting the black, red and gold Porsche logo. 'Is that enough for you?' he retorted disdainfully. 'I'll be less than ten minutes.'

As soon as Dubois had gone Ben and Sarah apprised one another of what had taken place before Ben had reached the courtyard.

'Jesus, I thought I'd lost you.' Gently placing her foot on his chair, Ben moved to where Sarah was sitting and threw his arms around her as if he would never let her go. Sarah returned his hug in equal measure. Eventually he retook his seat with her foot on his lap, speaking hurriedly. 'I couldn't find the street you texted me. It wasn't on the map. I ran around asking people; some didn't know and others sent me all over the place. I ended up a long way from the square, so I called you. When you didn't answer I was worried out of my mind. Then when you told me where you were, I found it. The fucking phone had autocorrected your text. Are you truly okay? What happened?'

Sarah told him. 'Dubois was trying to warn me off. He said my parents had lied to protect me.'

Ben listened silently until Sarah had finished. 'Well, we know they lied about Suzette having died, so he has a point. And he's right, we don't know what we're getting into here. If your folks lied about their daughter being dead, they must have had a bloody good reason. Although he's not confirmed it, Dubois hasn't denied kidnapping Suzette, has he? And we seem to be facing the conclusion that Jake and Lena were complicit, willingly or not. I mean, what kind of parents wouldn't report a kidnap? Only perhaps those who've been involved and, or, must protect their remaining child.'

Sarah shook her head slowly, bewildered. 'I don't know what to think. They brought me up to value honesty; why couldn't they be honest with me about this? Why couldn't they trust me?'

'Exactly,' replied Ben. 'They couldn't, therefore there must be a significant reason. Dubois implied that exposing the truth would be bad for you but worse for your mum and dad. Look, we can choose to think well of them, or decide that they're not the people we thought they were and we can't trust them. Either way, if we carry on pursuing Suzette it seems someone's likely to get hurt and we've no idea how or why. On the other hand, I understand that too much has happened for you to simply resume your life and the relationship with your folks. You need to think carefully.'

'One of the reasons I love you, Ben, is your pragmatism. I always believed I had a loving family and though I'm not so sure about that now, at least I have you. I know how much you value family. For you, life is uncomplicated—obviously I appreciate it wasn't always—but nowadays there's good and bad, prudent and reckless, happiness and despair, family and no family. The situation we're in now doesn't sit easily in any one category. If I have to choose between my parents and my sister, how would I do that? They're all family. If I choose one over the other, will I regret it? If I don't find Suzette, I'll always be wondering. It's so complicated.'

Ben leant towards her, the tone of his voice adamant. 'You don't have to tell me that life is complicated. Life is full of tough decisions. I put my past behind me in pursuit of fulfilment and happiness and look at me now: I have both. To say that was difficult is a massive understatement. It seemed impossible but I did it. I can't know what it feels like to have a twin you've never seen—an unimaginable pull, 1 would think. All I'm saying is try to make decisions with your head as well as your heart. If Dubois continues to caution, listen to what he has to say before deciding what to do. Then let's talk about it. We don't know him, Sarah. We don't know anything about him except we think he's capable of kidnapping a baby. How will we know whether he's speaking the truth? He might tell you upsetting things. The situation might get more confused. We don't know. All I know is I want you to be safe and happy and I'll do whatever I can to protect you.'

Sarah listened to Ben, her eyes glistening. 'I know one thing. I love you and I'm never going to let you go.'

He squeezed her hand. 'I love you too and you'll always have me in your life.'

The waiter came with a basket of bread. Sarah was retrieving painkillers from her bag when Dubois reappeared carrying two simple walking sticks and a paper bag from the pharmacy. He placed the bag on the table and hung the sticks over the back of Sarah's chair. 'I thought these would be useful,' he grunted.

'Thank you,' nodded Sarah.

She ate a piece of bread and swallowed two tablets with a glass of water while Ben expertly bound her ankle.

Dubois inclined his head towards her foot. 'You've done that before,' he remarked to Ben.

'I work in a gym, we have to know first aid,' he replied shortly.

Dubois poured them all a glass of rosé and took a large sip from his. 'I 'ave to warn you again, Sarah,' he said quietly, observing her, 'once you know something you can't turn back the clock. The truth you seek affects a lot of people, even you, Ben.' He turned his head and stared into Ben's scrutinising turquoise eyes.

'I understand,' replied Sarah. Her tone was calm, but inside her stomach was churning. 'But the thing is, how can I make a judgement about whether to know something if I don't know what it is?'

'Are you 'appy with your life?' asked Dubois.

'Yes.'

'Do you love your parents?'

She paused. 'Yes.'

'Do not underestimate the value of that 'appiness. Knowledge touches people, often in unexpected ways. Do you truly want to drag up the past and disrupt other people's lives and their 'appiness?'

Sarah shot a look at Ben. 'I came here to find my sister,' she answered determinedly. 'I'm not leaving until I know what happened to her and where she is.'

Dubois heaved a sigh. 'You might think you will gain a

sister but at what price?'

'The truth is the most important thing to me. You say this affects a lot of people—surely that must depend on what I do with the truth.' Sarah paused, her mind racing. She glanced at Ben again before turning back to Dubois. 'If Ben and I choose to do nothing with the knowledge then only we are affected.'

Dubois snorted derisively. 'You are wrong,' he stated resolutely, 'the truth will 'ave inconceivable consequences that you will not be able to control. I told you; your parents are implicated too.'

Their meals arrived, with more bread, the plates and basket borne expertly on the arms and hands of their waiter. He disappeared and returned with another water jug. Ben had been downing glasses of the lemon-laced liquid to dilute the wine to ensure he stayed hydrated and clear-headed.

'So be it,' Sarah declared, gingerly removing her foot from Ben's lap. 'I'm prepared to face the truth, whatever it is. I can't live a lie and pretend Suzette doesn't exist.' She took Ben's hand. 'Is that alright by you?'

'I'll support you whatever you do,' he replied gently. 'Whatever comes our way, we'll tackle it together.'

Ben turned to Dubois and fixed him with a hostile look. 'Can you guarantee no one will be physically hurt?' He lowered his voice further still, ensuring his words could not be heard by other diners. 'We're not going to be blackmailed, you know,' he asserted. 'And if you or anyone else threatens to harm Sarah, I will personally kill you. Do you understand?'

Sarah had never seen Ben this way although she was aware of violent acts of self-defence in his past. She knew he meant every word and a flush of anxiety rushed through her body. It was brave of him to face up to Dubois. Neither knew what the man was capable of. He hadn't denied the crime, the taking of her sister, yet he was trying to turn them away, to cut them loose. What might he do after that? He was demanding they trust him but was that just part of a plan? She needed proof Suzette was alive and well and that Dubois knew her.

'Can you show me a photo?' she demanded. 'Show me a picture of you with Suzette. When did you last see her?'

'Three weeks ago,' he replied, 'before my trip to England.' He pulled out his phone and swiped some photos. 'There,' he spoke curtly, handing her the phone. 'Now can you trust me?' Then he added softly, 'I'm very fond of 'er.'

Sarah gasped. The woman in the photo could have been her: the same blonde spiky hair, the same hazel eyes and freckles, the same small, slightly upturned nose. She even had the same smile. She was looking at herself but with no recollection of being in that place, with that person, wearing those clothes and smiling for the camera. She experienced a weird, out-of-body feeling, as if she were looking down on herself from a height. Suzy's world seemed entirely different from hers; a parallel existence in an isolated orbit. She knew nothing of her sister's life; her encounters, accomplishments, motivations, memories. What kind of childhood had she had? Had she had a party on her fifth birthday? Had her parents taken her to ballet lessons and tennis matches? Had she enjoyed wild camping and climbing windswept mountains? Had she got unbelievably drunk at her first over-sixteen party? Who had looked after her? Who had shared in her joys and comforted her in times of sorrow? Was it the man smiling with her in the photo, the man sitting not three feet away across the table? Sarah was flooded with resentment towards Dubois. Suzy had been ripped from her parents, deprived of her twin and given another identity. She wasn't living the life she was born to, that she was meant to have, but one filled with imposters. They should have grown up together, knowing everything about one another; learned and laughed and cried together. They should have been inseparable. Sarah felt an immense yearning to be with her twin.

She passed Dubois' phone to Ben, who studied the photo carefully, looking for any sign it might have been photoshopped. Suzy and Dubois stood close to one another, each with an arm around the other's back. Suzy was short and slim like Sarah. He zoomed in to look at the detail of the woman's face. The only difference he could see between the woman in the photo and Sarah was that the woman didn't have lowlights in her hair. He moved the enlarged picture around on the screen with his forefinger and spotted another difference. Suzette—he was sure it was her now—had a small dark mole on her collarbone. 'Thank you,' he said, passing the phone back to Dubois.

'Eat before it spoils,' Dubois uttered, motioning to the hot food in front of them.

The smell of rosemary, garlic and warm mushrooms rising from the table was too much to ignore. Sarah knew she must eat something more substantial than bread, if merely to soak up the wine. She had to keep a clear head, especially having taken painkillers, but the wine was delicious and was having a relaxing effect on her which she badly needed. The quiche was warm and delicious and its slightly soft interior melted at once in her mouth.

They ate in silence, each engaged in their own contemplation. Dubois finished his meal first and sat quietly staring into his glass of blushing liquor, deep in thought. Finally, he took a large gulp of wine, looked up and heaved a sigh. ''Ave it your way,' he said matter-of-factly. 'I agree to tell you everything. But we 'ave to do this my way and not 'ere. I can't 'ave you storming into other people's lives, uncontrolled. We take this step-by-step.'

Ben nodded his acquiescence and Sarah began to cry softly.

After lunch they walked slowly back to the car park, Dubois leading the way. Sarah managed quite well with the two walking sticks while Ben carried the shopping, keeping an arm free in case she stumbled. When they reached their hire car Dubois shook his head. 'We go in my car,' he declared.

Sarah and Ben looked at one another aghast.

'It's my way or nothing,' Dubois reaffirmed. 'If you're still afraid I might abduct you, tell someone where you are. Not your parents, Sarah,' he added sternly.

'Trust works both ways but understood,' replied Ben, in a worried tone. 'We still have a choice,' he reminded Sarah.

'Jen and Adam,' was her answer.

Chapter Eighteen

Cahors, France, 3 June 2018

Ben retrieved their bags from the hire car and locked it.

'It'll be safe 'ere,' Dubois told them.

On the way to Dubois' car Ben texted Adam to inform him briefly of what was happening. He followed it with a picture of the Porsche's number plate. "If there's any way of checking this out", he wrote, "would be grateful if you could do so".

Once settled in the car and on the road, Ben asked where they were going.

'Cahors,' Dubois replied, 'it's one and a 'alf 'ours from 'ere.'

'Is that where you live?'

'Thereabouts. I live outside the town.'

'Is that where Suzette is?' asked Sarah hopefully.

'No,' answered Dubois impenetrably.

Sarah continued to probe. 'Did you bring her up?'

'Bring 'er what?'

'Raise her,' Ben interjected. 'Did you act as her father?'

'No,' Dubois retorted, scowling.

Ben turned and darted a look at Sarah. She knew they'd both had the same thought—*that's one theory out of the window*. Sarah leaned forward from the backseat. 'Can you at least tell me what she's like?'

Dubois' face softened. 'She's like you—'er looks, 'er mannerisms,' he gave a short laugh, raising his eyebrows, ''er determination to get what she wants out of life. But she's also kind and gentle and thoughtful.'

Ben looked around at Sarah tenderly. 'And perceptive and loving and clever,' he added.

'Yes, that too,' remarked Dubois. He looked at Sarah in his rearview mirror. 'What do you do?'

'I'm a scientist. I studied chemistry at university. I work with governments and the oil industry to help prevent and clean up oil spills.'

Dubois half smiled as though he was not surprised. 'Suzette studied biochemistry and cytology.'

Sarah felt warmer inside. It was comforting to know they were both interested in science.

'Where did she study?' she asked, hoping to obtain a lead, something to help her trace her sister online.

Dubois didn't reply.

She wanted Dubois to divulge her sister's married name but sensed it would not be forthcoming. Instead she said, 'What does she do?'

'Cytologist,' Dubois responded impassively then turned on the radio.

It was clear from Dubois' closed expression he wasn't going to answer further questions about Suzette. Sarah's ankle had begun to throb again. There was little room in the back of the Porsche and their bags were on the seat next to her, but she managed to wriggle around to cock her knee over the seat divider and get her foot off the floor, placing a coat under her lower back.

Ben noticed her trying to get comfortable and twisted

in his seat to look at her. 'You okay?' There was more room in the front, but Sarah guessed he wouldn't want to swap places in case Dubois tried anything. Ben would be able to protect her better from his position.

'Ankle's hurting, but I'm alright.'

'Do you want another painkiller?' asked Dubois, 'I 'ave some water.' He reached into the side of his door and passed Ben a small plastic bottle.

'Yes, thanks.' Sarah took the water from Ben and rummaged in her bag for a tablet.

'Maybe try to sleep for a while,' Dubois suggested. 'It's another hour from 'ere.'

'Then what?' She spoke for them both, anxious to know what Dubois' plans were.

'Then, I take you to a place—a public place—where we can talk undisturbed. It's a neutral location and you will feel safe there. Then I will tell you what you want to know.'

No one spoke during the remainder of the journey to Cahors. The radio was on low, a program mainly playing music from the '80s and '90s. They passed between verdant vineyards, fertile pasture, flourishing sweet corn and fields of young sunflower plants growing eagerly skyward in anticipation of the summer sun. They drove through old Bastide villages of sunny limestone houses— some rendered and painted, some in their natural state— past pretty pigeonniers and castellated chateaus. The hills became steeper and the road more winding as it cut through thickly wooded slopes. Leafy woodland began to dominate, interspersed with small patches of meadowland. As they neared Cahors the road began to follow the sweeping curves of the River Lot as it cut through a basin with peaks on three sides. There, in the middle of an oxbow meander, nestled the old town.

The traffic became heavier as they passed through the modern outskirts. As they approached the urban centre the road ran alongside a section of the ancient city wall and soon they were on a nineteenth-century main thoroughfare. Shops and restaurants lined the street, which was fringed with plane trees. Tall, elegant buildings wearing pretty muted colours were interspersed with grand municipal creations: a college, the courthouse, the town hall and theatre. Locals and tourists were enjoying the afternoon sun, exploring, relaxing outside cafés and walking down to the river with their children for boating and swimming. Gazing out of the car window Sarah observed parents holding hands and cheerful looks on children's faces. She wondered bitterly what secrets might be hidden behind these happy expressions; what might be waiting unknown to darken the futures of these youngsters.

They passed an expansive open square furnished with an impressive fountain, then turned into the medieval quarter.

'This is the old city,' remarked Dubois. It was the first time he'd spoken in an hour and his voice was taut. 'I'm taking you to the cathedral. We can talk there.'

They drove through a labyrinth of narrow streets, interconnected with alleyways and entrances to cul-de-sacs and courtyards leading off. The area was crammed with old narrow red-brick and half-timbered buildings, galleried merchants' dwellings, stone archways and shady squares framed by pastel-painted houses.

As they drew nearer to their destination, Sarah's

thoughts became increasingly unsettled. She was close to the moment she'd longed for, when she would finally learn where her sister was and what had happened to her. She should be feeling excited, but a pool of dread had gathered in the pit of her stomach and was rising, as dense fog over stagnant water, choking her confidence and sinking her usual buoyancy. Dubois' warnings echoed through her mind. *You might think you will gain a sister but at what price? It would be worse for you, much worse. The truth will 'ave inconceivable consequences that you will not be able to control.* She reached forward to touch Ben's shoulder over the back of his seat and he placed a hand on hers in silent support.

Ben could almost touch the intensifying tension between Sarah and Dubois as the moment of truth came ever-nearer. He aimed to relax the atmosphere. 'This is a beautiful place. How old is Cahors?'

Dubois responded in an even tone. 'It 'as Roman origins but it came to be a wealthy commercial trading place in the twelfth century,' he paused, 'until the 'Undred Year War with the English.'

'Ah,' replied Ben.

'The cathedral was begun in the early 1100s then enlarged over the next six 'undred years,' Dubois continued. 'It is beautiful. There is a garden in the middle where we can sit undisturbed.'

'I'm looking forward to getting out of the car and stretching my back,' Sarah remarked casually. Ben wasn't fooled. He sensed that anxiety had swallowed her positivity; she'd want to get the next hour or so over with. He admired her courage and felt an overwhelming desire to hold her close, to comfort her.

They pulled into a square, in which resided several flourishing trees. At one end stood the striking Romanesque-Gothic cathedral crowned by two large domes.

Dubois parked the car in the shade. 'We 'ave until seven,' he stated.

Ben looked at his watch. It was nearly four o'clock.

They entered through a great arched doorway surrounded by elaborate stone carvings. Inside it was cool and quiet, the shadowy interior suffused with multi-coloured light emanating through a multitude of stained-glass windows. Fourteenth-century frescos adorned one of the vast domes. There were more centuries-old frescos on the walls, joined by a number of framed Renaissance paintings.

Dubois faced the altar and crossed himself before he walked towards the choir. 'This way.' He beckoned to Ben and Sarah.

They followed him to a side door to the right of the choir which led to a magnificent gothic cloister enclosing a garden laid out in geometric style. Clustered, carved stone columns fanned to spawn the many ribs of the vaulted ceilings and pointed archways; sculpted shells and intricate stonework resembling lace proliferated.

The garden was deserted apart from the three of them. A portion of the area was in sunshine while the remainder was shaded by the thick stone walls. A few wooden folding chairs had been placed on the paths between rows of low shrubs for people to sit in contemplation. Ben helped Sarah to sit on a section of the cloister wall, leaning against a pillar with her foot raised on the wall in front of her. The two men pulled up chairs and sat in a close circle with Sarah, comforted by the sun's warmth.

Dubois spoke quietly, necessitated by their location and the subject. Sarah and Ben followed suit.

'You must allow me to tell you this story my own way.'

'Of course,' responded Sarah and Ben nodded.

'I mean no questions, no interruptions, until I've completely finished,' Dubois continued sombrely.

'Okay,' replied Sarah hastily.

Ben realised she was so anxious to hear what Dubois had to say that she would have agreed to almost anything at that point.

'I mean it—this is very important. You will 'ave many questions and most of them will be answered by what I 'ave to say so please listen, no matter what you 'ear, until I'm done.'

Ben squeezed Sarah's hand. 'We'll do as you say,' he responded for them both.

Sarah wet her dry lips with her tongue. She was trying to keep her expression calm, but knew Ben could see the stress in her eyes. 'Please, go on.'

Dubois acknowledged their acquiescence with a nod, took a deep breath and began. 'I met Mari, the woman you accosted in the car park in Plymouth, in 1983. She's a… friend. The man your friend spoke with in the clinic, Pierre, 'e's also a friend. We were at college together. Mari and your mother were also friends, although I didn't know your parents. Do you know anything of your parents' life in Plymouth?'

'Not much.' Sarah's voice was cracked. 'They didn't talk about it, except for their childhoods.'

Dubois reached into his jacket pocket to produce a small bottle of water which he passed to her.

'I understand they were very 'appy,' Dubois continued, staring at the gravel beneath his feet. 'But there was a point at which everything began to go wrong. 'Owever, I must go further back.'

Chapter Nineteen

The cloister garden was in complete shadow once Dubois had finished imparting the truth of the situation.

Sarah's face was ashen and her cheeks were stained with tears. Her throat had dried and her hands shook as she took a sip of water—now warm and tasting of plastic—so she cupped the bottle between them to steady herself. Ben had been squeezing her hand intermittently as Dubois related his account, but she had hardly noticed it, her mind crazed with a multitude of emotions. She found it impossible to think clearly, to process the information she'd received. She stared at the gravel at the base of the wall on which she sat, moving her head from side to side as disbelief fought to overcome devastation, hurt, anger, betrayal and naked vulnerability. Her entire world was collapsing and she struggled to keep the pieces together, denial her mind's natural protective mechanism.

Ben and Dubois remained quiet for a time.

Finally, Sarah spoke. 'Mum and Dad wouldn't do that.' Her mouth was set determinedly and her eyebrows drawn. Repudiation and wrath were her first reactions. 'No,' she shook her head again and looked Dubois in the eyes, 'you're wrong. You've had hours to think this up. You stole my sister and now you've come up with some fucking convoluted crap to justify it.'

'Why the 'ell would I take your sister unless for the reason I've told you?' Dubois countered indignantly. 'Not for a ransom, as you well understand. And 'ow likely is it that a Frenchman would kidnap a child in Scotland just because 'e wanted a baby and 'e didn't 'ave one, huh?'

Ben gently laid a hand on Sarah's arm, shooting Dubois a nervous look. Sarah could tell he was also shocked to the core, but his gesture told her the words Dubois had spoken made sense to him, although he looked as though he was reeling from their blows.

Ben held a palm towards Dubois. 'Give us a minute,' he uttered in a moderating tone. They exchanged a look of mutual perception. Dubois got up and marched off.

'Sarah, love,' Ben ventured cautiously, 'the events leading to the kidnap that Dubois has recounted... they do seem to explain why your parents hid all traces of Suzette and avoided telling you the truth; why they left Ullapool so suddenly without telling their friends; why there was no death certificate for Suzette and no report in the press about an abduction.'

Sarah couldn't think straight and needed somewhere to direct her fury. The stranger who'd abducted her sister and was now trying to brainwash her with his insidious lies was some way off, across the other side of the garden. And the one person she thought she could always rely on for support seemed to be taking his side. She shook Ben's hand off her arm. 'You believe him,' she spat.

'God, Sarah, I don't want to,' Ben shook his head sympathetically, 'but what other explanation could there be?'

She didn't want to believe Dubois. To believe him was to lay herself open to injury—a turtle on its back, helpless against the fisherman's spear. But she felt like she'd already been pierced and the wound was opening up, spreading, threatening her with destruction. She began to cry again.

After a while she became aware of Dubois who had returned and was standing a few feet away.

'I think we need time,' Ben remarked kindly, directing his comment to the Frenchman while regarding Sarah tenderly. 'Come on, sweetheart, let's get you off this wall and somewhere more comfortable.' He stood, one shoulder lowered so Sarah could reach around his neck for support while she gingerly lifted her swollen ankle and shuffled so that she could reach the ground with her good foot. 'We need to find a hotel,' he said over his shoulder to Dubois.

'I'll make a call,' the man returned quietly.

He drove them to a thirteenth-century château ten kilometres from Cahors, situated high on a limestone cliff overlooking the River Lot. They approached the impressive, fortified castle, the central building guarded by imposing cylindrical towers at the outer corners topped with grey conical roofs. Though stunningly beautiful, they could not possibly afford to stay. Ben said as much to Dubois.

Dubois shrugged. 'It is taken care of. It's the least I can do. It's peaceful 'ere; no traffic, beautiful views, tranquil gardens. You can take the time you need. You will not be disturbed. Ask reception for anything you need.'

Ben nodded his gratitude. With difficulty and the use of the walking sticks—Sarah would not accept any aid from Dubois—Ben extracted her from the Porsche. She hobbled towards the sweeping stone steps leading across the dry moat to the château entrance. She hadn't spoken since they'd left the cathedral and longed to be out of Dubois' company.

In a daze, she allowed herself to be assisted into the castle by Ben and a friendly porter, through a long gallery past tapestries and ancient portraits and up a wide shallow staircase. Their spacious room, decorated in dusky pink and mink, was flooded with the light streaming through tall French doors leading to a balcony overlooking the luxuriant Lot Valley. Ben helped her onto the expansive double bed and rang room service for a hot drink and a brandy for her and a whisky for himself.

Sarah lay on the bed, sinking comfortingly into the velvety covers, while Ben busied himself around her. After a short while he placed a warm cup into her hands and she tasted strong, sweet tea. She was feeling nauseous as wave after wave of emotion swept through her body, churning her stomach, her mind flooded with myriad thoughts, overwhelmed and unable to reason. Over the last couple of hours an earthquake of words had collapsed her entire world: she was not who she'd thought—she didn't know who she was anymore. If her mum and dad could betray her like this, what else was a lie? Her whole life felt like a forgery. All of a sudden, her parents seemed alien, disconnected and disengaged. The unwanted separation clawed at her, ripping her heart like the body of a lamb in an eagle's talons. She desperately wanted to turn back the clock, to unknow the known. But now the truth of the situation had been revealed, she finally had to admit Dubois' account did seem to offer and validate explanations for the various mysteries presented over the last month. Suzette hadn't been kidnapped as much as "illegally recovered"; taken to be reunited with her genetic parents. And those people, those French strangers, were her parents too.

Sarah felt an upsurge of faintness swell and ripple through her body so that her arms and legs quivered weakly, her throat constricted and she almost lost consciousness. The earthquake had reduced her life to rubble and she was choking on the dust.

Later that evening as they lay in bed, Sarah curled into Ben's shoulder and the crook of his arm, they spoke softly.

Ben was trying to engender a constructive mood or, at least, to keep her from falling into a pit of depression. 'One positive thing to come out of all of this is that you have a twin sister who is alive and well. You'll be able to meet her. She'll have to be told and it's bound to be hard for her too—I guess that's something you'll share from the outset.'

Sarah wiped away another tear. She couldn't seem to keep them at bay. 'I don't know who I am any more. I feel lost. Apart from you, Mum and Dad were the people I most loved and trusted in the world. And now...' her voice, weak and vulnerable, tailed off into nothing.

Ben shifted, withdrawing his arm from her shoulder to look her in the eyes. Tenderly moving a strand of hair aside, he bent to kiss her forehead. 'You're the same person you always were—exactly the same. You are you! You always have been and you always will be,' he emphasised. 'Knowing yourself comes from within. You've always been strong-willed and independent; you've always been logical and brave. You fight for what you believe, make your own decisions in life and live by them.' He shook his head.

'That doesn't change.'

'But I feel different,' Sarah sobbed. 'I feel… alone… like an astronaut on a spacewalk whose line has just been severed. I'm floating around, unable to get back to Mum and Dad.'

'Listen to me,' Ben responded earnestly, gripping her upper arms, 'Lena is still your mum. She carried you inside her for nine months and gave birth to you. Her blood is running through your veins. She and Jake brought you up, fed and clothed you, educated you, laughed and cried with you, looked after you when you were sick, encouraged your ambitions, supported you through life's ups and downs and, above all, they love you—beyond words. They wanted you, Sarah, more than anything in the world; you heard what Dubois said. I was abandoned. I have no parents. To have people close to you, who love you that much… well… you can't put a price on that, believe me.'

Sarah nodded slightly and sighed resignedly. 'You're right,' she snuffled, 'I know Mum and Dad love me and, deep down, I know I still love them, but I feel so conflicted. Mum's blood may be in my veins, but we're not genetically related. I resent them; I'm appalled at what they did and they deceived me—my life has been a lie.'

It was Ben's turn to sigh. 'I understand only too well how you feel. I was resentful because I felt unwanted. But the resentment eats away at you then you push everyone else away too. I ended up resenting all my foster carers because they couldn't cope with me and in my distorted mind it seemed that each of them had discarded me which made the bitterness grow even more. It's a dangerous cycle. I read somewhere recently that harbouring resentment is like taking poison yourself and expecting the other person to die. It can never do you any good. Try to be angry, rather than resentful. Anger can be vented; anger dissipates—if you let it. You need to focus on one strong emotion to be able to work through it.'

Sarah snuggled back against his warm solid body and he drew his arms around her, stroking her hair and kissing the top of her head. He was her haven; she felt safe with him and she knew she could draw on his energy. His words made sense. She realised just how angry she was, but the anger gave her strength and would help her to put her other, more vulnerable feelings to one side for the moment.

'Let's try and get some sleep,' Ben murmured. 'I'll call Dubois in the morning and tell him you want to meet Suzette—when you feel ready for that of course.'

'Yes, I definitely want to see her,' a ripple of fear swept through her, 'if she agrees to see me.'

'I'm sure she'll want to meet her twin sister as much as you did when you first found out about her.'

'I hope so. But then… I'll probably have to meet her par… my real…' Sarah found she couldn't quite speak the word in its new context. Instead, an equally problematic image came to mind and she heaved a trembling sigh. 'Oh God, then I have to confront Mum and Dad.'

She felt Ben's comforting squeeze. 'Let's just take one day at a time,' he whispered calmly.

She hugged him back. 'Love you.'

'Love you too, sweetheart.'

Ben eventually fell into a slumber, but sleep wouldn't come to Sarah, exhausted as she was. She lay on her side, swollen ankle uppermost, struggling to empty her mind but it refused to quieten. The depths of the night heightened her deliberations and emotions, distorting and exaggerating them. Dejection and defeatism seeped into her confused consciousness, allowing negativity the upper hand. At around half past three, when she felt she'd reached rock bottom, she rose quietly and hobbled towards the window with the aid of her sticks.

Moving belongings to one side to perch on the cushioned window seat, she caught sight of the photo of her and Suzy playing with Moira's little girl in Ullapool. Ben had given it to her shortly after they'd returned home from Scotland. She'd been grateful to have it then and had kept it close ever since. She concentrated on the picture, trying to force her mind back to that time, desperate to recall any contact with her twin. It upset her that, apart from the traumatic mental image of Dubois with Suzy bundled up in his arms, she couldn't remember being with her sister, only the name, Ouzi, that she'd given to her imaginary friend when she was alone.

She continued to stare at the toddlers in the old print and suddenly a connection was made in some deep recess of her memory, evoking a sound: Ayah. She repeated it to herself and tried adapting the syllables to make sense of it; ayah, ay-ah, say-ah, sar-ah. Realisation struck; it had been Suzy's name for her.

At last she felt able to calm her thoughts. Gazing out at the pewter moonlit river and hearing the faint screeches of owls in the nearby woods, she imagined the scene in the shadows before her. Owls were calling to their mates as they hunted; carp would be resting in the calm stretches of the river; wild boar feeding on acorns and walnuts; red squirrels sleeping in their drays curled up with their young; wall lizards guarding their eggs under rocks and in dry stone walls and the grapevines on the other side of the water would be sprouting their tentative green shoots. She could see the twinkling lights of Cahors in the far distance, settled amongst the hills. Life prevailed all around her, triumphing and enduring. She set her jaw determinedly. She would not be sunk by Dubois' revelation. Nature renews and regenerates.

So would she.

Chapter Twenty

Saint-Cirq-Lapopie, France, 5 June 2018

The road twisted through the steep-sided valley, marking the cut of the gentle river Lot. Dubois had turned up to collect Sarah and Ben in his Renault, which had been much easier for Sarah to climb into, although her sprained ankle was a good deal better and the swelling had reduced significantly. Ben and Dubois were chatting in the front of the car. Dubois' demeanour had improved considerably since he'd left them at the hotel two days ago; today he appeared the embodiment of equanimity and Ben's manner in his company had eased considerably in response. In contrast, Sarah was as taut as the strings of a racket; trepidation had flooded her body although she had tried to suppress its control of her mind. She sat in the back, hands clasped, the fingers of one hand tapping nervously on the knuckles of the other. For the last month she had been pursuing this moment and now it was imminent she felt fearful, though of what she couldn't describe. She stared out of the window, trying to focus on the scenery to allow her body the chance to relax.

Here and there the valley opened, gently sloping fertile land on either side of the river hosting small enclosures of pasture and crops. However, for much of the journey the road shadowed the grey-blue ribbon of water in the lee of a massive limestone cliff, occasionally entering a tunnel cutting through a rocky outcrop. Eventually they crossed a bridge and began to climb, snaking this way and that until, around a sharp left-hand bend, their destination came into view.

The medieval village, situated a hundred metres above the river and dominated by an impressive Gothic fortified church, cascaded down the cliff-side, a jumble of charming steeply-curved, brown-tiled roofs accommodating tiny dormer windows. They followed the road as it continued to curve upwards around the edge of the settlement until they reached a parking area set into the heavily wooded cliff-top. Then they wound their way down through a maze of narrow paved lanes, cobbled alleyways and attractive squares, among a multitude of half-timbered and mullioned houses, underneath stone arches and past the ruins of an old fortress.

Dubois—he now insisted they call him Xavier—had explained that Suzy's husband Gabriel rented a woodturning workshop and gallery in Saint-Circq-Lapopie during the spring and summer seasons and generally stayed in the accommodation above his studio, as he often worked in the evenings. Due to her shift work at the hospital, Suzy split her time between there and her apartment in Cahors.

Gabriel's house was situated at the lower end of the village, the gallery, accessed through arched half-glazed double doors at the front, displaying a collection of items beautifully crafted from wood. On the left was a set of stone steps leading to a small balcony and the floor above. A gated passageway to the right led to a small courtyard and workshop at the rear of the cottage. The courtyard was half covered by a metal frame over which clambered a purple wisteria. In the shade underneath, sitting at a round table, was Suzette.

Sarah halted in her tracks for a few seconds. It was astonishing to come face to face with her duplicate, to look at another and see her own eyes, her own nose, her own smile. Suzette was a complete stranger but so much a part of her. She was shaking with euphoria. Then a strange, comforting calmness came over her. *My twin soul*, she thought, *my twin heart. You complete me.*

With eyes glistening, she stepped forward, smiled and managed to utter a timid, 'Bonjour.'

Suzette, tears spilling down her cheeks, jumped up, strode across the flagstones, grabbed her hands and kissed her on both cheeks. 'Oh, *mon Dieu*. Hello, Sarah, *ma précieuse soeur!*'

Sarah was suffused by an overwhelming need to embrace her sister. She threw her arms around Suzette, who responded similarly, exclaiming '*Merci, merci*,' over and over.

As they hugged, Sarah whispered, 'Ouzi.'

'Ayah,' Suzy responded softly.

We hope you have enjoyed reading *The Search*

Book 2 of *The Identity Thieves Trilogy* continues with

The Choice

You can read the first chapter while you await the continuing story:

The Choice: Chapter One

Plymouth, England, 30 May 2018

Mari drove from the waterside inn to a quiet residential side street in West Hoe, squeezed her Mercedes between two parked vehicles and cut the engine. Fear tumbled and lurched in her stomach and her hands were shaking. The fact she'd been accosted and screamed at was unnerving in itself, but being confronted by Suzette's mirror image in such a hostile manner alarmed and distressed her. The woman's obvious anguish clawed at Mari's heart—*Tell me where Suzette is! She's my twin, for God's sake!*—while guilt and anger flooded her senses.

Mari fumbled around in her handbag for the pack of cigarettes she kept there for emergencies. She'd been trying to quit but hadn't been able to let go of her backup support. She found the packet and took out a cigarette, shoving it in her mouth while she felt around for the lighter, which evaded her fingers. 'Fucking hell,' she shouted. In a fit of pique she tipped the bag's contents onto the passenger seat. Having lit up and inhaled deeply a few times, she ran one quivering hand over her hair, tidying stray wisps behind her ears and patting her French twist, trying to steady herself.

Her hands were still trembling as she reached for her phone and saw she had a couple of missed calls from Xavier. She dialled his number and his phone diverted to voicemail. *Bloody hell*, she thought anxiously, *he's in the meeting, he could be hours.* She noticed she had a voicemail herself and listened to the message. It was from him.

He spoke with urgency. 'Mari, listen, we need to talk. My meeting should be finished within a couple of 'ours. Can we meet straight after that? I know we'll see each other this evening but this cannot wait. Text to say where you'll be and I'll join you.'

She rested her elbows on the steering wheel and put her head in her hands for a moment, trying to think clearly. Ash fell onto the upper sleeve of her green cotton blouse and she raised her head, brushing it off quickly. Her mind was whirling with thoughts and questions. She tried to catch hold of one and deal with it before moving on to the next.

If those women had noted her in Malvern with Xavier and had also been at the inn where they'd had lunch today they must be pursuing either her or him. Had Suzette's sister actually tracked her to Plymouth or had she been hunting Xavier and encountered her, for the second time, by chance? Mari came to the conclusion they were following her, since Xavier was in France most of the time.

It was obvious now the woman who'd approached her in the ladies' room of the eatery, speaking about Xavier, wasn't a private investigator working for her husband. But, she reflected, her initial assumption had been understandable given Gerren's increasingly resentful behaviour over the last few weeks and that had originally unsettled her. Now she knew she was being hounded for a far more ominous reason. A quiver of panic emerged from the knot in her stomach and began to flutter.

Mari had only seen Suzette once, in London with Xavier, but the likeness was undeniable. It shocked Mari to her soul to hear the woman talking about searching for her sister. Thinking about it sent fresh waves of dread through her body, making her limbs go cold. She began to feel slightly lightheaded and wished she had brandy to hand. It couldn't be, after all this time, could it? Christ, it didn't bear thinking about, yet here she was, trapped in a thirty-year old tragedy. All those years apart from the man she truly loved and, just as they'd found one another again, their past was threatening to catch up with them.

Myriad emotions swept through Mari, disrupting her reasoning and displacing her rationality. Her feelings tumbled around, dust in a wind storm: immense love for Xavier, yet anger at him for the intrusion of his family into her life once again; resentment at Gerren for the years of bland soulless marriage; bitterness at having convinced herself comfortable monotony was better than any alternative; anxiety at the possibility of losing her home; dread of what might come to pass in the following days if those women continued to pursue them. Her whole life seemed to be on a cliff edge.

Mari lit another cigarette and tried to still her mind.

The nicotine had the effect of enhancing her dizziness as she hadn't smoked in a while. She wanted to go home, to lock the door behind her and shut out the world, to sit with a refreshing gin and tonic on her secluded terrace in the sunshine, gazing quietly over the water. But she knew something had to be done and first she would need to talk with Xavier.

She looked at her watch. Xavier would probably be another hour in the board meeting with Pierre. She tried Fran again. On hearing Fran's bright tones Mari uncharacteristically burst into tears and it was some moments before she could speak properly. Between sobs she told her friend everything that had happened since she'd left Fran a voicemail on exiting the restaurant: that Suzette's sister had approached and grabbed her arm; how the other woman had stopped her from closing the car door; how they'd questioned her over Suzette's whereabouts and accused her of lying—she had been lying, of course, and the frightening thing was they knew this and seemed to be following her.

Fran confirmed she'd received Mari's earlier message about the stranger trying to find out how well Mari knew Xavier and she'd sent Pierre a text, telling him to warn Xavier. She spoke calmly and slowly. 'Listen, Mari, don't panic. Go around to the back of our house and put your car in the garage. The key is in the usual place. There'll be room for Pierre's car as well and I'll park on the road. In case anyone's tracking Xavier—I'm not saying they are but in case—I'll warn Pierre to conceal Xavier in the back of his car. They can drive in and shut the gate and no one will be able to see Xavier, or you for that matter, entering the house. We can all talk about this later and decide what to do. Okay?'

Listening to Fran's even, composed voice made Mari feel slightly better. She imagined the tone Fran had used was normally reserved for dealing with worried clients in Chambers. She was reminded she didn't have to handle any of this on her own; the four of them would always support one another—the promise they'd made. 'Thanks, Fran,' she sighed gratefully, 'what would I do without you?'

'You never have to thank me, you know that. Anyway, we're all in this together, one way or another,' Fran responded wryly.

Xavier lay low in the back of the Maserati as Pierre drove. Worry had, long ago, drawn lines between his eyebrows and he felt these creases deepen with resentment and anger. *Merde!* Here he was, after three decades, having to hide like a bloody criminal. He tried to calm himself. That much was true, technically, but he'd only done what he knew was right.

Inside Pierre and Fran's elegant four-story Georgian home, overlooking the Tamar estuary and Mount Edgcumbe, Pierre went to the kitchen to make coffee while they waited for Fran. As Xavier entered the living room Mari ran to him like a child and he gathered her in his arms, holding her tight against his body and stroking her hair.

Mari spoke agitatedly, staring past Xavier at the polished wooden floorboards. 'For a moment I thought I'd seen Suzette again. Her sister is so like her. She's following me, Xavier, she's bloody stalking me! She kept asking me about Suzette. She tried to stop me from driving away. She actually put her hand on my arm.' She gave Xavier an anguished look. 'Then she screamed at me. Christ. I had to get out of there.'

Xavier was visibly shaken, but his tone was controlled. 'I saw 'er too this time, out of the car window as we were leaving the car park. There's no doubt it's Suzette's twin.'

'Did you mention…?'

'No, of course not.'

Mari momentarily covered her mouth with one hand. 'She sounded so desperate. Her scream; it tore through me,' she said, moving her head slowly from side to side.

Grim determination showed on Xavier's face and he spoke as if through clenched teeth. 'Pierre 'as 'er registration number.' E's asked Fran to check 'er details.'

'Can she do that?'

'She's a barrister, remember. She 'as… connections.'

Mari turned to the window. The Cornish coast across the estuary was bathed in sunshine. 'Do you remember that day?' she murmured.

Xavier's eyes followed Mari's and his face softened fleetingly with the recollection. 'We all visited Mount Edgcumbe; I've never forgotten it—'ow could I? It was the day I fell in love with you.'

Mari continued to stare out over the water and her voice took on a distant quality. 'Knowing what you know now, would you do the same again?'

Xavier sat down on the little window seat in front of her, cradling his head in his hands, reflecting. Eventually he raised his head and shrugged. 'We all did what we thought was for the best.' He paused. 'Would you?'

'So much fallout; so many consequences; so many lives affected,' Mari uttered sadly. 'No… I wouldn't. We should have left it to the professionals.'

'Do you mean taking the child or… right from the beginning?'

'The beginning, the Lesters, everything,' she answered.

Xavier grabbed her hand. 'Listen, Mari, you only ever tried to 'elp.'

'Yes, but what good did it do? It wrecked us, didn't it?'

'I'm going to take care of this,' Xavier urged, anger surging through his words like the Severn Bore, swelling second by second. 'I'm not going to lose you all over again.'

The living room door opened and Fran walked in. Pierre followed close behind with a pot of coffee and four mugs, which he placed on their smoked-glass coffee table, returning to the kitchen for warm home-made banana bread. They gathered on the two large mink velvet damask sofas, facing one another across a generously-proportioned and exquisitely-woven Persian rug. The aromas of fresh coffee, banana and warm sultanas drifted comfortingly between them.

Fran smiled thoughtfully at Mari and Xavier as she poured the coffee and indicated they should help themselves to cake. 'Between us we will deal with this,' she stated resolutely.

Xavier nodded his agreement and Mari managed a half-smile.

'First, we have to establish beyond doubt it was definitely Suzette's twin sister,' instructed Fran, thumbing through emails on her phone. 'You two are obviously sure. Pierre obtained the car registration number and I've had it checked out. Mmm… yes… here it is.' She looked up to find the others all staring intently at her in anticipation of the verdict.

Fran took a deep breath. 'The Toyota Prius being driven by Suzette's doppelganger is registered to a Sarah Lester,' she pronounced.

'I knew it,' declared Xavier. 'Sarah was the name written on the other cot.'

Fran looked at Xavier empathetically. 'The address recorded in association with that registration is in Malvern, Worcestershire,' she continued.

'Well that makes sense,' Mari stated, 'as it's where I saw her first.' She turned to Xavier. 'Today she said she knew you and I had spent a weekend there. It was as if she was threatening me, wanting me to know she'd been following me. How the fuck did she find us here? How long has she been pursuing us? I mean, what does she actually know?'

'I can't believe 'er parents would have told 'er anything,' Pierre stressed, 'knowing what they 'ave to lose.'

'Per'aps they've lied to 'er,' suggested Xavier bitterly, draining his mug of coffee and refilling it. 'Per'aps they told her a story with the characters swapped around.'

'We're assuming Jake and Lena are both alive and well,' Mari pointed out. 'They're a similar age to us, so I expect they are, but who knows. I mean it's possible Sarah discovered something about Suzette following their deaths; documents, diaries maybe.'

'They'd 'ave been bloody stupid to write anything in a diary,' Xavier expressed disdainfully.

'A deathbed confession maybe?' Mari suggested.

Fran raised a hand to halt the discourse. 'As far as I can tell, both of them are alive,' she affirmed soundly.

Xavier and Mari looked at their friend in surprise.

Pierre indicated his head towards his wife. 'She's

always a step a'ead,' he smiled.

'They're both on the full electoral register,' Fran explained, 'though their address details aren't on the open register. I checked this afternoon.'

'Going back to what Sarah may or may not be aware of; only six people know for definite it was Xavier who took Suzette,' Pierre said assuredly, taking another piece of cake. 'Whatever the Lesters may 'ave told Sarah, she couldn't 'ave found Xavier and Mari through any of us. If she'd discovered Alain, she'd 'ave found Suzette already.'

'It doesn't matter at this stage what she thinks she knows,' Fran stated assertively. 'She can have no proof of the kidnap. We have to decide what to do next. As far as I can see we have a number of options: we can do nothing and see what her next move is; we can warn her off; we can warn her parents off; or we could tell her the truth.'

'I don't think we can sit around doing nothing,' Mari answered edgily. 'At the very least Sarah will find out where we live and continue to pursue us. I'm sure of it.'

'Yes, we 'ave to stop 'er some'ow,' Xavier agreed, nodding determinedly.

'How would we warn her off?' asked Mari apprehensively, hugging a scatter cushion to her chest.

'I can't see what information of any substance she'd 'ave on any of us,' Pierre answered. 'So we could put the frighteners on, tell 'er if she continues to ask questions she'll get more than she bargained for. It's true of course.'

Xavier nodded his agreement. 'We can threaten unimaginable consequences. She doesn't know what she's getting into.'

Mari spoke quietly. 'I don't want her to be frightened. I just want her to go back to her life and leave us to ours.

If we tell her the truth, we'll expose ourselves and we'll hurt her and others. There's been enough damage. I think her parents should be warned off, anonymously of course, and they can deal with it.'

'I agree with Mari to a certain extent,' declared Fran. 'But we have to consider how we'd deliver a warning and we're making an assumption Jake and Lena have a good relationship with Sarah or have any influence over her. Another option would be to give Sarah a legal harassment warning. Although it may not be effective, it would serve to show her we're unafraid of her accusations. If that doesn't work then I might vote for warning the Lesters off. But...' she paused, looking at each of the others in turn, '... there's an elephant in the room here. Doesn't she actually have the right to know the truth?'

They all reacted at once.

'Jesus, Fran!'

'What?!'

'Are you serious?'

'Alright, alright, I'm simply putting it out there,' Fran responded, raising her hands. 'I think we should consider it as an option.'

'Yes, but there are huge consequences. How can we possibly tell her?' Mari answered, aggravated.

Xavier sensed Mari was looking to him for immediate support, but he avoided her eyes, instead staring down at his feet, buying time while trying to consider Fran's observation. *If it were Suzette, how would she feel?*

Pierre broke the silence. He spoke calmly, his initial disquiet at Fran's suggestion having subsided. 'I think I can see where Fran is coming from. What has kept us all safe all these years?' he asked rhetorically. 'The fact we're all in it together, the Lesters included.' He shrugged. 'They didn't report their child missing at the time—they moved, they disappeared. Why should it be any different now?'

'We're not dealing with the Lesters now though, are we? We're dealing with the daughter. We don't know what she might do. We don't know what she's been told, or what she's found out,' answered Mari forcefully.

'I'm not disagreeing with you, but we 'ave to remember her parents are implicated. Would she really want to expose them?' Pierre countered.

Xavier considered Pierre's question for a moment then shook his head. 'Maybe not; 'owever it would be a big risk,' he argued. 'We don't know 'ow she might react. She might want some kind of revenge. I can't be accused of kidnap.' *And I can't risk losing Mari.*

'Yes, it's not straightforward,' said Fran. 'If we warn Sarah off by emphasising her actions will harm her parents, that presupposes she loves them and cares what happens to them. Whatever their relationship in the past, she might now feel hate or resentment towards them. We certainly can't risk any kind of written threat which Sarah could take to the police.'

'I think the fact Sarah 'as started pursuing me after all these years implies something 'as gone wrong with our safety mechanism,' Xavier noted.

Fran spoke decisively. 'Right, I think we're all agreed telling her the truth is risky. So, I suggest we try and warn her off with a verbal threat of legal action on the grounds of harassment, for starters. I can deliver it.'

Pierre sighed discontentedly. 'I don't like the thought of you 'aving to engage with 'er. You're the only one of us she 'asn't seen.

'She won't know who I am. I'm merely a legal representative. I really think it's the best course of action at the moment. Okay?'

The others nodded their approval.

'But if she persists, we'll 'ave to deal with 'er in another way,' warned Xavier.

Later that evening, after dinner, Fran took Mari into her office in the basement. The sun, low in the sky, shone in through the glass patio door, filling the room with a diffuse amber glow. Fran unlocked the bottom drawer of her desk and took out a large brown envelope. 'I'm sorry,' she said, handing it to Mari.

Mari tore open the packet and removed its contents. Her features were stony as she looked through the photographs. She glanced up at her friend. 'When were they taken?' Her tone was cold.

Fran looked at Mari sympathetically. 'A few weeks ago... after you'd told me Gerren was backtracking on the house and beginning to make accusations. I... uh... know people.'

Mari nodded slowly and tapped her lips with an index finger. 'I can't pretend I don't feel anything,' she reacted, 'but we're both going our separate ways anyway. I guess his accusatory tone with me was because he's been trying to cover his own tracks. Where does she live?'

'She's actually in Noss Mayo. She's a divorcee with two grown-up kids.'

'Oh. The house looks nice,' Mari responded flatly.

'It has a view of the water.'

'So... he doesn't need mine then.'

'No.'

Mari put the photos back in the envelope and gave Fran a hug. 'Thanks.' She turned to leave the study but turned back, holding the packet aloft. 'Why these?'

'Insurance,' replied Fran.

As Mari was leaving the room Fran called after her. 'Everything's documented, you know. I mean... what happened before the Lesters left Plymouth. We have records. They're... locked away.'

Mari gave Fran a reluctant smile. 'I wouldn't expect anything less from you,' she said.

Acknowledgements

I owe so much to my talented creative writing mentor, Tracey Iceton, for her vision, inspired editing and constructive encouragement, without whom I would not be in this position. I am also eternally grateful to Cinnamon Press, for awarding me the opportunity to work with Tracey and for seeing something in my writing and being willing to give me a chance.

At Cinnamon, I owe a great deal to Jan Fortune for her warmness and support and for guiding me through the publication process and to Adam Craig for his beautiful cover illustration. At Leaf by Leaf, huge thanks to Rowan Fortune for his patient editing.

A special thank you to the readers of the very first draft before it was teased apart and reconstructed into books one and two of this series, Manfred Evans, Becky Baker and Sally Sutton, for their invaluable comments and positive feedback. I'm also grateful to my friend Carine Monetti for her help with French swear words (and, of course, the other translations)!

To my lovely husband, Andy, my deepest thanks for his unswerving support and belief in me.